BEGUILING THE DUKE

LORDS IN LOVE

BOOK ONE

DARCY BURKE

Beguiling the Duke

ISBN: 9781637261064

This is a work of fiction. Names, characters, places, and incidents are the product of the author's imagination or are used fictitiously. Any resemblance to actual events, locales, or persons, living or dead, is purely coincidental.

Book design: © Darcy Burke.
Book Cover Design © Dar Albert, Wicked Smart Designs.
Editing: Lindsey Faber.

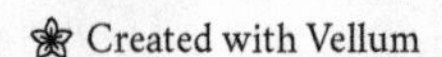

For Elyssa, the bestest beta reader and a fabulous friend

BEGUILING THE DUKE

On the way to meet his future wife, the Duke of Lawford's coach loses a wheel. Repair is impossible because he's landed in Marrywell on the first day of their annual May Day Matchmaking Festival and *everyone* is on holiday. Furthermore, there are no rooms to let, so Law must accept the hospitality of a country squire or, more accurately, from his beautiful, clever daughter who obviously runs the household.

After a disastrous foray at the matchmaking festival four years ago, Sadie Campion has mostly hidden away at home. But at twenty-four, this may be her last chance to marry and have a home and family of her own. When her unexpected houseguest offers to help her attract a husband, she can hardly refuse and, on the duke's arm, becomes the belle of the festival.

As they grow closer and attraction simmers between them, Law wonders if *she* is the match he was destined to make...

Don't miss any of **Lords in Love**!

Love romance? Have a free book (or two or three) on me!

Sign up at http://www.darcyburke.com/join for members-only exclusives, including advance notice of pre-orders and insider scoop, as well as contests, giveaways, freebies, and 99 cent deals!

Want to share your love of my books with like-minded readers? Want to hang with me and get inside scoop? Then don't miss my exclusive Facebook groups!

Darcy's Duchesses for historical readers
Burke's Book Lovers for contemporary readers

CHAPTER 1

May 1816
Marrywell, England

Sadie Campion marched across the damp ground after dropping a loaf of Mrs. Rowell's fresh bread at Sadie's eldest brother's cottage. He hadn't been at home—he was out in the sheep pasture with their father—and his wife had been chasing their three-year-old son around the parlor while clutching the one-year-old boy on her hip. That had prompted Sadie to take her youngest nephew and amuse him for a good half hour so his mother could have a respite. But now Sadie was behind in her regimen for the day.

Quickening her pace, she glanced up at the gray sky. "Don't you rain again. Or at least do me the courtesy of waiting until after I clean the front door. I'd rather not have to add changing clothes to my list of things to do."

Sadie strode to the front of the house where she'd placed the broom and ladder that she planned to use outside the door. When she reached the porch, she put her basket down and set the ladder in place. She plucked up the broom and climbed the ladder, frowning at the cobwebs that had been there for too long now. But what was she to do? There simply wasn't enough time in the day for her to complete everything that needed to be done.

Though her father would balk and say he didn't want to spend the money, Sadie needed to talk to him about hiring at least one more person to help. It didn't have to be a housekeeper, though that would be nice, just someone who could take on a variety of tasks that never seemed to be completed because there weren't enough people at Fieldstone to do everything.

Working quickly—both because she was behind, and she was now slightly irritated by her father's obliviousness to how hard she worked—she didn't look to see if there was anything living in the webs. So when the spider landed on her forehead, she yelped. She also let go of the ladder and lost her balance, falling backward.

Panic flashed through her. She didn't have time to be hurt!

Instead of hitting the ground, she landed on... someone. The large figure didn't quite catch her, but his strong arms came around her. "Careful," a masculine voice murmured near her ear.

His deep tone and solid form against her back soothed her. She inhaled his sandalwood scent and felt a stirring of awareness as well as curiosity. This was obviously not one of her brothers or her father. Nor was it their groom or the land manager. Who, then, was it?

Sadie turned to see an astonishingly handsome gentleman she'd never clapped eyes on before. Tall and white with deep-set eyes the color of walnuts and lips that were surely too full for a man, he regarded her with concern. His features were strong and patrician, with a prominent brow and a square jaw, and he looked to be about thirty years of age. He wore a stylish hat, but she could just make out blond hair beneath it.

"Why on earth are you climbing a ladder without assistance?" he asked, sounding a trifle annoyed as his brows pitched down over his eyes. "What if I hadn't been here to catch you?" His presumptuous questions dispelled the enchantment that had come over her.

Sadie took a step back, clutching the broom. The gentleman wasn't alone. There were two other men standing just beyond him. One, who was a few years older than the rude Adonis, cradled his left arm and wore a pained expression. He possessed a snub nose and thick, dark brows. The other man was perhaps twenty years older than the man who'd caught Sadie. He had a long nose and a sharp chin. His cravat was perhaps the most intricately tied neckcloth Sadie had ever seen.

"Who are you, and why are you here?" Sadie asked pertly, even as her body still tingled from where her body had touched his.

"He is the Duke of Lawford, and you should mind your tone," the older man answered, his dark gray brows pitched into an angry V.

The blond man shot a look toward the older man before addressing Sadie. "Our coach has lost a wheel. My coachman has injured his arm, and my valet knocked his head."

Sadie gasped. "You lost a wheel? Goodness, you are all lucky you weren't more seriously injured."

"I'm fine," the older man insisted as he continued to glower at Sadie. She looked back toward the "duke." Was he really a duke? Perhaps they weren't more badly hurt because the accident had never happened. Indeed, this entire scenario seemed highly unlikely, and it would be just like her brothers to play a joke like this. Sadie narrowed one eye at Adonis. "How do I know you're a duke? And did you really suffer a mishap?"

"Of all the impertinence!" the older man snapped, his eyes flashing in outrage.

The supposed duke exhaled. "If it's not too much trouble, Mrs...?"

"Miss Campion."

The duke's eyes widened slightly as if he found her unmarried state surprising. Perhaps he did. As a woman of twenty-four, she was practically on the shelf.

"Miss Campion, I am indeed the Duke of Lawford. If it's not too much trouble, might we borrow a vehicle to continue to the nearest town so we may find a physician and someone to repair my coach?" the duke asked.

Oh dear, it sounded as if he had no idea where they were. Or when.

"Ah, why don't you come inside?" Sadie said, summoning a smile as she was about to ruin their day even more.

"I don't wish to trouble your employer," the duke said smoothly.

Her...what? He likely thought she was a maid. Or the housekeeper—perhaps that was why "Miss" instead of "Mrs." had surprised him. As housekeeper, she would be Mrs. Campion, whether she was married or not. Sadie glanced down at the mud on her hem from walking across the estate earlier and didn't have to touch her head to know that a great many curls had escaped her chignon. It was more than believable that she was an employee at Fieldstone instead of the daughter of the owner.

She didn't take the time to disabuse the duke of his assumption. "You really need to come inside... to sort things out. Please allow me to offer you some refreshment, and I'll send for the doctor. Marrywell isn't two miles down the road." She gestured west with the broom.

"Marrywell? I am not familiar with it," the duke said with authority. "Perhaps someone can drive us into town to see the doctor? Then I can hire a coach to continue driving us to our destination."

The man was likely used to getting his way. She gave him a bland smile. "If you'll just come inside, I'll be happy to explain why none of that will be possible, unfortunately."

The duke blinked, and his blond brows arched. "I beg your pardon?"

"You've arrived on the first day of the Marrywell May Day Matchmaking Festival. No one is available for hire to drive you anywhere, and I daresay there won't be anyone to repair your coach. Not until the festival concludes. In a week. We could take all of you to town in our, ah, carriage or the much sturdier cart, however I think you will be more comfortable waiting here while the doctor is alerted to your needs."

The older man—the valet, Sadie deduced—stepped forward. "That is unacceptable. This is the *Duke of Lawford.*"

Goodness, did the man think the duke was some sort of deity?

Sadie tried one last time. "Please come inside, at the very least so your coachman can rest."

The duke's gaze flicked toward the house, a sprawling, several-times-expanded farmhouse that lacked a uniform style. One might call it "charming" or "quaint." She could only imagine what an esteemed peer thought of it.

"It sounds as if we'll need to secure lodging," the duke said with a slight frown.

Sadie gave him a sympathetic look. "I'm afraid that won't be possible either. Every inn within a ten-mile radius will be booked to the rafters for the festival. Please, just come inside. We can discuss your options while your coachman rests."

The duke turned his head to the man holding his arm. "Come, Holden, let's get you some tea."

"Thank you, Your Grace." The coachman winced as he moved forward, and Sadie noticed he was also limping.

Sadie hastened to move the ladder. While she set the broom down first, however, the duke picked up the ladder and moved it out of the way of the door.

"Thank you," she murmured, adding, "Your Grace." She picked up her basket and opened the door, gesturing for all three men to go inside.

Walking into the entrance hall, she led them on through the staircase hall into the parlor. She'd never been embarrassed of her home, and she still wasn't, but she had to think their modest domicile was not up to ducal standards. The furniture was well cared for, but certainly not new, and the room, as a whole, didn't pretend to possess any sense of style.

Sadie held out her hand. "Please sit wherever you'd like. I will have our groom run into town to fetch Dr. Bigby."

The coachman sat carefully in a chair and the valet on the settee while the duke remained standing. "*Your* groom?" Lawford asked. "Who are you exactly?"

Before she could respond, her father and eldest brother, Esmond, burst in.

"Damn me, there's a wrecked coach on the

road!" Esmond blinked his jewel-green eyes at the three visitors.

Sadie's father, Winchell Campion, glanced toward the duke and his men, his brown gaze cautious and perhaps even judgmental. "Sadie, who are these gentlemen?"

"Father, Esmond, allow me to present His Grace, the Duke of Lawford. That is his coach on the road."

The duke's eyes narrowed slightly as he regarded Sadie with a sudden blatant curiosity. "Your father owns this estate?"

Sadie gestured to her father and then her brother. "Yes, this is Winchell Campion, owner of Fieldstone and squire. This is my eldest brother, Esmond."

"Your wheel came clean off!" Esmond said excitedly, sweeping off his hat to reveal his dark brown curls. "I bet that scared the piss out of you!" He laughed jovially, and Sadie stared at him.

Their father jabbed an elbow into Esmond's side. "That is no way to greet a duke. Or anyone else, for that matter."

Esmond straightened and schooled his features into a more serious expression. It was an astonishing transformation and one that typically only their dear departed mother or Esmond's wife could provoke. "Welcome, Duke," he said.

"It's 'Your Grace,'" Sadie said softly. "Father, we need to fetch Dr. Bigby. The coachman's arm is injured, and the valet hit his head."

The duke pivoted toward her father. "I said we could call on the doctor in town since we have to find lodging. However, your daughter has indicated this will not be possible."

"No, it will not," her father said with a laugh.

"There's nary a room between here and Winchester."

"Then we'll hire a coach to drive us to our destination," the duke said, as if Sadie hadn't already explained that wouldn't be possible. Did he not believe her?

"I told him that wouldn't work either." Sadie didn't bother hiding her exasperation.

"Listen to Sadie," her father said. "She knows what's what, and you won't find a more clever girl."

"She mentioned you have a carriage. I would pay you handsomely if we could borrow it. I'll have it returned as soon as possible."

Sadie's father laughed. "That carriage barely makes it to Marrywell and back. No, no, I'm afraid I couldn't allow you to risk yourselves, especially not after the bad luck you've already experienced. Indeed, there's no vehicle at Fieldstone that will suffice. Do not despair, however! You'll stay here. We've plenty of room, especially since Philip wed a few months ago." He referred to Sadie's other older brother, who, like Esmond, lived in a cottage on the estate.

"We couldn't impose," the duke said tightly.

Her father walked to him and clapped him on the shoulder, oblivious to the duke's eyes subtly rounding. "You must, and that's all there is to it. Your coach is in dire need of repair, and you won't find anyone to fix it until after the festival. Is your, er, wife with you?"

The duke's aristocratic jaw clenched as he looked down his nose at Sadie's shorter father. "I do not have a duchess. When, pray tell, will the festival conclude?"

Sadie had also told him that detail. Had he heard nothing she'd said? She pursed her lips at him in annoyance.

"In a week." Sadie's father looked positively delighted.

"That is unacceptable!" the valet snapped.

"It is *unfortunate*," the duke murmured.

While Sadie's father might be pleased to host the duke, Sadie found him arrogant. As well as attractive. No! That didn't signify. "Can't Jarvis repair the coach?" she asked. Jarvis was their retired groom and coachman. He lived in a small cottage on the estate.

"We can't ask him to do that, not with his arthritic hands," her father protested.

"Perhaps he could advise Esmond and Philip, and they could do the actual work," Sadie suggested. "I'm sure Adam and Richard could help too." Those were her younger unmarried brothers.

"I can direct them," Holden said. "Can't do much with my arm like this, but mayhap tomorrow, I can instruct them on how to repair the coach." He shifted in the chair and promptly grimaced. Sadie felt certain he would hurt even more tomorrow and would need to rest.

"Yes," the valet said quickly. "We must do whatever is necessary to see His Grace on his way at the earliest possible moment."

"Yates, everyone will do their best, but our accident has occurred at an inopportune time," the duke said to the older man, sounding beleaguered. Lawford then shifted his gaze to Sadie. "I would appreciate if you could enlist whomever you can to work with Holden to complete the repair. I'll pay you for the work and whatever you need." The duke looked to his coachman. "I can help you if necessary."

Yates appeared horrified. "You *cannot* perform manual labor. They *must* have a coach we can borrow," he insisted.

Lawford swung his gaze back to Sadie's father, but it was Sadie who responded. "We do not have a vehicle sufficient for your needs. Our coach is old and...well, it's inadequate for long trips." Decrepit was the best description, but Sadie wasn't going to say that.

The valet appeared thoroughly outraged. "But His Grace has important business that he *must* attend to."

Yes, well, Sadie needed to not have her orderly life interrupted either. She thought of all the tasks that weren't getting done while she dealt with this crisis. And would continue to deal with if they hosted a very important guest for a week. Not to mention how their arrival would affect her plans to attend the matchmaking festival. The welcome reception was that very afternoon and set the stage for the entire weeklong event. All young ladies seeking to be matched attended the reception, as well as the May Queen, who chose seven of those ladies to be maidens fair. The queen and her court were the focal point of the festival, and being a maiden fair meant almost certain betrothal by the end of the festival. At twenty-four, Sadie was the same age as the oldest maiden fair ever chosen. This year was her last chance to find a husband—to have a home and family of her own.

Sadie needed to finish her chores so she could get ready. "I'm sure my brothers—with Holden's or Jarvis's instruction—can manage the repair, and you'll be on to your destination in no time. Mayhap even tomorrow."

Her father shook his head vigorously. "Impossible. Replacing the wheel will take a few days at least."

Yates opened his mouth, but the duke held up

his hand toward him while keeping his focus on Sadie. The older man pressed his lips together.

Their maid Mavis came in and glanced around the room with interest.

Sadie had meant to ring for her, but things had been too chaotic. She moved next to Mavis and spoke quietly. "This is the Duke of Lawford and his coachman and valet. Their coach lost its wheel, and they'll be staying with us for…a while."

"Bad luck for them unless they're happy to attend a matchmaking festival." Mavis grinned, then her gaze settled on the coachman. "I wouldn't mind if he came along," she whispered.

Ignoring the maid's saucy observation, Sadie continued, "We need rooms prepared and a tea tray. Are you terribly busy helping Mrs. Rowell?" Their cook made the cakes for the welcome reception, and they were likely in the middle of boxing them all and loading the cart.

"Gwen and Bryan can keep helping her," Mavis said, referring to the other maid, who primarily assisted Mrs. Rowell in the scullery, and Mrs. Rowell's son, who was their groom.

Sadie grimaced. "We need Bryan to summon Dr. Bigby. His Grace's coachman has hurt his arm, and his valet hit his head. But if you're all leaving soon to set up at the reception, he can just take care of it then."

Mavis shook her head. "I'll send him now."

"And Gwen should bring tea," Sadie said.

"I'll let her know." Mavis waggled her dark brows. "Nothing like a bit of excitement on the first day of the festival!"

Sadie didn't want this kind of excitement when she was trying to get her chores done so she could go to the reception!

Mavis looked to the coachman, who was

wincing at that moment. "He looks to be in pain. I'll get his room sorted straightaway." She left the parlor with haste.

Sadie addressed their guests. "We'll have tea in a few minutes, and hopefully, the doctor will arrive within the hour. Your rooms will be ready shortly. Is there anything else we can do for you at the moment?" Sadie was desperate to get on with the things she needed to complete before the reception, but wondered if she ought to stay and entertain the duke. She dearly hoped not.

"I don't suppose you could see about removing my coach from the road?" the duke asked.

"Of course." Sadie turned her head toward her father and brother. "Papa? Esmond?"

"Yes, yes," Papa said. "Esmond! Fetch your brothers and move His Grace's coach."

Sadie should have realized her father wouldn't help. He much preferred to direct, and even then, he was content to let Sadie manage nearly everything.

Before Esmond could go, the duke stopped him. "Mr. Campion, if you also wouldn't mind bringing our cases to the house since we are to be...staying here, I would be most appreciative."

Esmond nodded. "Right away, My Grace."

Wincing inwardly, Sadie hoped the duke hadn't noticed that her brother didn't know the slightest thing about proper address. Sadie wasn't sure *she* knew all the rules.

The coachman, Holden, stood abruptly. He clenched his jaw and clutched his injured arm more tightly. "I must retire. Doesn't matter if a room's prepared. Do you have something in the stables?"

"I'm afraid not," Sadie replied, hating to see the man in pain. "You should be in the house anyway, so the doctor can examine your arm. We'll have your room ready in no time. In fact, I'll go see to it." That would get her out of the parlor so she could finish her chores.

Pivoting, she left the room but was stopped in the staircase hall by her father, who'd followed her. "Where are you going?"

"To help Mavis prepare the rooms. That should have been obvious since I said as much."

"I mean, why are you leaving *the duke*? You need to stay and entertain him."

Sadie looked down at her attire and tucked a loose curl behind her ear. "Am I garbed for entertaining? No. I'm dressed for chores. Please let me complete them before I need to prepare for the reception."

"You're going?" he asked, surprised.

"I'm sure I mentioned it."

"I would have remembered," he said with misplaced certainty. "You've only attended—as a potential bride—once. I thought you never meant to return."

That *had* been her intent after the disastrous first year she'd attended the festival as a potential bride. Sadie brushed the memory away. She couldn't afford to let it occupy her mind when she was, in fact, hoping to use the festival for what it was intended—to find a husband. "I'm twenty-four, Father." Sadie was out of time, which was why she *needed* to attend the reception this year. "Don't you think it's time I wed?"

"In fact, I do," he said, shocking her. He'd never shown the slightest interest in her marital prospects. He was content to have her here managing Fieldstone's household. "And we must thank divine intervention for the arrival of a duke on our doorstep." He grinned, his dark eyes dancing with excitement.

What on earth was her father doing? "I would appreciate you not matching me with the duke. That isn't even within the realm of possibility."

"Why not?" he asked, sounding petulant. "You are pretty and capable. I wager you could manage his ducal estate with ease."

She stared at him, wishing he expressed appreciation of her skills when there wasn't a duke involved. "Then consider this: I don't *want* to manage his ducal estate." The idea of wedding a duke was preposterous. She wouldn't know the first thing. "I'm going to the reception, where, if I am lucky, the queen will choose me to be crowned one of her seven maidens fair tonight." That was Sadie's best chance of making a match. The maidens fair were the most sought after by the bachelors seeking to wed.

Her father appeared nonplussed. "Why do you need to be a maiden fair or even attend the festival when you have a duke *right here*?"

Sadie exerted considerable effort not to roll her eyes. "I'm going to prepare the rooms, then do the rest of my chores. *You* entertain His Grace. And do *not* play matchmaker. He's a duke and I'm a…I don't know what I am," she muttered.

She marched up the stairs and met Mavis in the corridor. The maid carried a stack of linens. "I was just taking these to His Grace's chamber. Then I'm going to run up and take care of the room for the coachman and valet."

"I can make the duke's bed," Sadie offered, taking the linens. "Put the coachman and valet in the room at the end of the corridor." It was the largest on the second floor and had two beds. Only two rooms on that level were occupied—by Mavis and Gwen. Mrs. Rowell lived in a cottage on the estate with her husband and their son.

"That was my thought as well," Mavis said. She inclined her head down the corridor. "The duke will be right across from you."

Sadie briefly closed her eyes. "You aren't going to play matchmaker like my father, are you?"

The maid, who was a few years older than Sadie and had been with the household for over five years, smiled as disbelief flickered in her gaze. "That's surprising to hear, but I suppose it's not every day a duke lands on one's doorstep."

"What is it about a duke that makes everyone atwitter?" Sadie mused.

"Come now, don't tell me you don't find him handsome," Mavis said with a sly smile.

She did, in fact. And arrogant. Shaking her head, Sadie walked past Mavis feeling disgruntled.

Everyone viewed the arrival of a duke as some sort of splendid opportunity for Sadie, but to her, it was a massive imposition. She liked order and routine as she had a great many things to manage on a daily basis. This week, she'd planned on attending the entire festival for the first time in four years, and now that was in jeopardy because of the additional work having the duke here would bring.

She would just have to make do. This was her last chance to be chosen as a maiden fair, which would all but guarantee she would wed. Then, she could manage her *own* household and have her *own* family.

If not, she'd become the Spinster of Fieldstone. And life would pass her by.

CHAPTER 2

John Holbrook, the Duke of Lawford, could just barely stand at his full height in the bedchamber assigned to his valet and coachman. Thankfully, they were several inches shorter than he was. Holden sat propped up on his bed, while Yates occupied a chair. The valet wore his usual sour expression, but it was more pronounced today.

Dr. Bigby had left in his small, two-person gig a short while ago after prescribing rest for both men along with a tonic for pain. Holden's arm was badly sprained, and the doctor indicated he shouldn't drive for at least a week. He also needed to rest, so he would not be able to help with the coach repair, at least not tomorrow.

"It seems as though we are trapped here at Fieldstone for the duration of this silly festival," Yates said with considerable rancor. "If my head did not pain me, I would walk as far as necessary in search of a coach for us to flee. We should at least find a way to get word to Lord Gillingham to explain our tardiness." The valet sniffed, which was his favorite wordless expression of distaste.

Law had managed not to think of the purpose

of their journey since the wheel had come off. Now, he realized just how pleasant that had been. Not the accident, but not thinking of his impending betrothal to a young lady he'd never met. "It sounds as if we won't have luck finding anyone to deliver a message. A week's delay isn't that bad."

"Your father would think it was," Yates grumbled. He never failed to remind Law of what his father would do or think. Law excused the nuisance because Yates had been his father's valet for more than thirty years. It made sense that he was incredibly loyal to the former duke, and Yates was particularly invested in ensuring that Law's father remained a steadfast presence in his son's life, even from the grave.

He was also correct. Law's father would have had many thoughts about this entire affair. He would have demanded the Campions drive him to town, and he would have bullied his way into an inn, displacing whoever had the misfortune to stand in his way. Then, he would have used the same overbearing demeanor to compel someone to either fix his coach or drive him to Dorset to meet Gillingham. Law couldn't bring himself to do those things, but he had tried to press for different results with Campion despite his daughter already telling them the futility of their situation. Law regretted doing that.

Law didn't respond to Yates, whom he'd taken on after the duke's death when Law had promoted his own valet to succeed the retiring butler at the London house. While Yates might not have been the valet he might have chosen, Law didn't have the heart to release him after such a long tenure in the household. That was where he and his father had most differed—Law possessed a heart, though he'd worked to hide that from his father. Since his mother had died when he was fourteen, all his father's softness, which hadn't been a great amount, had disappeared. Law had wanted to meet—or exceed—every one of his father's demands in the hope that it would bring him some measure of happiness.

That was the reason Law found himself traveling to Dorset: to determine if he and a young woman his father had chosen would suit. As the duke had lain dying, he'd insisted Law vow to wed the daughter of his old friend, the Earl of Gillingham. Law had specifically said he would *consider* it. There was a reason he hadn't yet wed at the age of twenty-nine. He'd yet to meet a woman who moved him to want to.

His father had taken that as an agreement to wed her, however, and had dispatched a letter to Gillingham before dying, saying that Law would marry the man's daughter. Six months later, Law had agreed to spend a week with Lady Frederica to see if they would suit, but he feared the earl already saw the transaction as complete.

"Honestly, I'm pleased to have some additional time before potentially consigning myself to the parson's trap," Law said. Particularly if it meant spending time with the intriguing Miss Campion. She'd seemed utterly unimpressed with him, and after a lifetime of being told he was more important than nearly everyone else—which was absolute rubbish—he found that rather captivating. He also needed to apologize for his obnoxious behavior. He should not have doubted her, particularly since she was clearly the person in charge here.

Yates wrinkled his long nose. "You can't leave Lord Gillingham hanging. He was a dear friend of your father's. They've known each other even longer than I attended His Grace. It was of paramount importance to him that you join the two families. Indeed, your father never pressed for you to marry until Lady Frederica was nearing her debut—precisely because he wanted this union."

That much was true. When, at the age of twenty-four, Law had not demonstrated an interest in taking a wife—in truth, he simply hadn't found a woman he wanted to wed—his father had started to suggest Lady Frederica as his duchess. He'd said that if Law just waited five or so years, she'd be of marriageable age. Their ten-year age difference was of no consequence to Law's father.

Now, five years later, Law was indeed contemplating marriage to her. But only because his father had demanded he do so, and Law, as usual, had felt beholden to please his father, especially on his deathbed. Law supposed there was a chance they might suit, but he was not enthusiastic about an arranged marriage. The closer he got to meeting her, the more reluctant he became. This delay was a boon, and Law would seize it.

Law held up his hands. "I don't see that there's anything we can do. Don't trouble yourself. We'll just have to make the best of it. To that end, I don't want either of you discussing the purpose of our journey with anyone. Is that clear?" He pinned his gaze on Yates, for he was the one with a tendency to flap his lips, as he'd demonstrated earlier in the parlor.

"I wouldn't presume to speak of such things," Holden said.

Law arched a brow at Yates, who crossed his arms and pursed his lips. "I won't say anything either. I hardly see how it signifies."

"I would like to enjoy this unexpected...sojourn," Law said. "I'd prefer not to think of obligations, and I expect you to comply with my instruction."

Yates made a face that looked as though he'd sucked on a lemon. "If you insist."

"I do." Law often found Yates frustrating, but the man did as he was told, likely because his former employer, Law's father, wouldn't have tolerated anything else.

"If the coach manages to be repaired in the next few days, you could drive it," Holden suggested, thankfully changing the subject.

"Absolutely not!" Yates's blue eyes bulged. "He's a duke!"

Holden gave the valet a surly stare, but said nothing.

Law worried that they would be sharing a room. They were vastly different in temperament. Whereas Yates would raise his voice and assert his displeasure, Holden would suffer in silence and ignore most irritations. Law just wasn't sure how long the coachman could ignore Yates, who could be the biggest irritation of all.

"I happen to be a duke who can drive a coach, and I will if necessary. I will also assist with the repair if I am able." However, Law had warmed to the notion of staying for the week and postponing the introduction to his potential bride. "Furthermore, I am a duke who can unpack his own belongings, which I have already nearly completed." He gave Yates a smug look.

The valet, in turn, appeared horrified.

Turning, Law went to the tray the maid had delivered earlier. It held tea and biscuits and some pretty little cakes decorated like flowers and crowns. He picked up one of the cakes and took a bite. Almond and mace danced across his tongue. Swallowing, he waved what was left at Holden and

Yates. "If these cakes are any indication of the cook's talents, we are in for a culinary treat."

After eating the rest of the cake and tamping down the urge to devour what remained on the tray, Law went to the door. Turning back toward his retainers, he said, "You should rest—after you eat those cakes, of course. Yates, please take care of Holden since his arm isn't terribly mobile, and don't be gruff about it." He gave the valet his best ducal stare, then departed.

Taking the stairs down to the first floor, he paused as he saw Miss Campion walking from the chamber situated across the corridor from his. How...interesting to learn his room was so close to hers.

She looked quite different from earlier in the day when he'd mistaken her for the housekeeper. Her light brown hair had been restyled with no errant curls, which was a shame. He rather liked that aspect of her appearance. Actually, he'd found her quite attractive, and when she'd landed in his arms after losing her balance on the ladder, he'd felt her lush curves. He'd experienced a rush of heat before she'd moved away from him.

Her emerald gaze met his, and the nostrils of her small, button-shaped nose flared slightly. She walked toward him, and he gave her an appreciative nod. "Miss Campion. You look lovely."

She glanced down at herself. He noticed she'd done that earlier too, as if she were self-conscious about her garments. Instead of the earlier sober gown with its muddy hem, she wore a smart, rose-colored walking dress. He would not have mistaken this version of her for a servant.

In retrospect, he wasn't sure how he'd erred. She possessed an air of confidence and authority that he found most alluring. Hers was not the demeanor of an employee. No, *she* was the one issuing commands.

"Thank you, Your Grace. How are your valet and coachman?"

"They are doing well, thank you. I left them to fight over the delicious cakes on the tea tray."

Miss Campion smiled, and Law was struck by just how pretty she was. There was a genuine warmth and care to her that was so unlike most of the women he met in London. It wasn't that those women weren't genuine or warm, but that they didn't allow themselves to be when meeting a duke. He generally believed that when he encountered most people, he was, more often than not, interacting with an untrue version of that person. At least that was what he'd observed with his father over the years. He'd seen gentlemen behave a certain way in front of him and then in a more relaxed fashion when the duke wasn't there or paying attention.

"Mrs. Rowell does make the best cakes," Miss Campion said. "It's why she supplies them for the welcome reception. She started several years ago, and I wonder what will happen when she decides to retire from doing so."

Law noted that Miss Campion seemed more pleasant than earlier. Or, more accurately, less harried. "I do apologize for causing trouble with our arrival. It is most inconvenient of us to disturb your plans for the festival."

She blinked at him. "That is...thank you. It's very kind of you to say so."

"I also wanted to apologize for thinking you were the housekeeper." He realized he hadn't met the housekeeper and presumed they didn't have a butler. "Where is she, by the way? I should like to thank her for accommodating our intrusion."

"I'm not surprised you assumed I worked here. I certainly looked as if I do, and well, that's because I do. We do not have a housekeeper, and before you ask, there is also no butler."

Then it was no wonder she was left to clean the front door. Still, one of her brothers should have helped her. Or better yet, they could have done the task entirely. "It did seem as if you manage the household, but I didn't imagine you wouldn't have a housekeeper. Isn't that challenging?"

She shrugged. "We haven't had one since I was twelve, when Mrs. Evans died."

"I see." He wanted to ask more questions, such as where her mother was, but he assumed she too had passed away and didn't want to bring that up when Miss Campion was clearly about to embark on a social occasion. "Where you are going?"

"To the welcome reception for the matchmaking festival."

Law also wanted to ask more questions about the festival. Since he would apparently be staying here, he may as well make the most of the situation. He had an idea. "I've never been to a matchmaking festival. Perhaps I could join you?"

She hesitated. "Ah, yes, I suppose you could. I confess I'm surprised you would want to. I thought you were keen to be on your way to something important."

"Since that is not an option, I'm not going to spend my time fretting about it. I'd much rather learn about your festival. Would you mind if I just fetch my hat and gloves from my chamber?"

"Certainly. I'll wait for you downstairs."

"Oh, and I owe you one more apology," Law said. "I should not have doubted the information you provided me regarding our situation. You were trying to be helpful, and I was being...difficult."

She blinked at him again. "That's kind of you to say. Thank you. Now I feel as though I'm repeating myself."

"Well, I did apologize—necessarily—several times." Smiling briefly, he hurried to fetch his things, checking his appearance in the glass before running his fingers through his hair.

When Law arrived downstairs, Mr. Campion stood with his daughter. He wore a wide, expectant smile. "There he is! How splendid that you are driving Sadie to the reception."

Miss Campion narrowed her eyes at her father subtly and briefly, but Law caught it. What was that about?

"I didn't realize I was driving," Law said. "I thought your vehicles were insufficient."

"For a long journey yes, but our gig is perfect for two people and drives nicely. Go on now." Campion clapped his hands together. "Make sure my girl is chosen as a maiden fair, will you?"

Law had no idea what that meant, but said he'd do his best. Offering his arm to Miss Campion, he enjoyed the rush of anticipation her touch provoked. It was hard to believe that he'd awoken that morning with leaden feet, wishing he didn't have to go to Dorset to meet Lady Frederica. And now he was looking forward to attending a provincial festival with the pretty daughter of a squire, a young lady who was also basically a housekeeper. His father would be repelled. Perhaps that was why Law felt the opposite.

They went outside to where the gig was waiting in the drive. An older man of around seventy stood beside the single horse. He scrutinized Law for a moment before turning his attention to Miss Campion. His grizzled features softened. "Sadie, you are prettier than any maiden fair to ever be crowned."

Miss Campion laughed lightly, and the happy sound fluttered across Law's chest. "Thank you, Jarvis. This is His Grace, the Duke of Lawford. Did Esmond speak to you about his coach?"

"Yes. I stopped by the stables." He shook his head and looked at Law. "You're lucky you're walking about. That was a bad accident."

It had been rather frightening, and Law was certain that several parts of himself were bruised. "I do appreciate any assistance you can provide. My coachman can also offer guidance on the repair, though I doubt he possesses as much knowledge as you."

"He's also recovering from an injury," Miss Campion said.

"We'll take care of it." Jarvis gave Law a confident stare. "It'll take a couple days, especially with everyone so busy at the festival. I imagine the boys will be off most afternoons bowling or spending too much time in the brewer's field, but we'll manage."

"I appreciate it." Law handed Miss Campion into the gig, then circled around to get in.

She waved to Jarvis as they drove away, and Law didn't wait to begin satisfying his curiosity. "This festival really does monopolize everything, doesn't it?"

"It is the heart and soul of Marrywell. Where do you think the town's name comes from?" she asked with a wry smile.

Stupidly, he hadn't put that together. "The town was founded around the festival?"

"Yes, May Day celebrations were quite popular hundreds of years ago. Marrywell sprang up around one particularly successful festival that boasted a great many matches. It is the oldest May Day festival in England."

"Indeed?" Law was impressed. He turned onto the road, near where they'd lost the wheel. "If you don't mind, explain to me this maiden fair business. How am I to ensure you become one?"

"You can't, regardless of what my father said. The May Queen will spend the reception surveying all the young ladies who are looking to wed, then tonight, she will name seven maidens who will become her court for the duration of the festival. They will be crowned at a celebration in the botanical gardens."

"You wish to be crowned this evening?"

She lifted a shoulder, and he sensed a hesitation. Or perhaps a discomfort. "I suppose every young lady does."

Law didn't know her age, but she wasn't as young as someone embarking on their first Season. He would guess she was in her early twenties. Had she attended this festival many times and not made a match? He found that almost criminal, especially if this festival claimed to make a great many matches.

He tried to keep things light. "Here I thought the purpose of the festival was to find a match."

"It is—mostly—and being a maiden helps that along because those seven ladies become the most popular of the celebration. However, the festival is also just a wonderful time for everyone, with dancing, food, games, and so much more. The Grand Picnic on the middle day of the festival is not to be missed."

"I think I'm quite glad to have my business delayed," he said with a smile.

"What business is that?"

"I was to meet with someone about a potential...arrangement." That was a particularly cold way in which to refer to a betrothal, but in this case, it fit. If there was to be a match between him and Gillingham's daughter, it would be entirely arranged as a transaction. If Law managed to like Lady Frederica into the bargain, so much the better. However, given that she was chosen by his father, he didn't expect that to happen.

Moreover, he didn't want to go through with the marriage if he wasn't drawn to her in some way. What sort of marriage was that? Even his obnoxious father had loved Law's mother.

"I hope your delay won't cause trouble for you," she said.

Law was actually hoping it would. Perhaps Gillingham would declare him feckless and call the arrangement off. "I'm sure everything will work out as it should," he said benignly. "Now, do tell me how I can help you become a fair maiden."

CHAPTER 3

Sadie looked askance at Lawford. Was she really riding to the welcome reception with a duke? Apparently so. This was nearly beyond comprehension.

More than that, he was turning out to be pleasant and mayhap even...charming. Earlier, she'd found him imperious and haughty. When he'd offered to escort her to the reception, she'd hesitated. But then, saying no would have been rude.

Plus, he'd seemed more relaxed. He'd even complimented her. She'd wondered if he actually meant it or was simply offering a platitude. Gentlemen like him were skilled in empty flirtation. Sadie knew that from experience.

Except, she should not compare him to Osborne, the man who'd flirted with her most expertly at her first festival as a marriageable young lady four years ago. He'd been a singular blackguard. Not that she could prove that assertion since she hadn't allowed herself to get close to another gentleman since. It was easier—and less humiliating—to focus on managing Fieldstone.

She wasn't even entirely sure she wanted to be a

maiden fair. All that attention and fuss...but it was her best chance to wed.

"Miss Campion?" he prompted, reminding her that he'd posed a question. He glanced over at her, and a tremor danced across her flesh, which had also happened when he'd handed her into the gig. It had also occurred when he'd caught her earlier as she'd lost her balance. She reasoned this was normal since it wasn't every day that she was this close to a handsome gentleman, let alone a duke. It had to be normal to feel an odd thrill, didn't it?

"I don't know that there is anything you can do to *ensure* I am chosen. There are no rules. The queen just chooses seven young ladies."

"That seems rather arbitrary."

"I suppose, but I doubt the queen would agree. Each queen puts her own thought and reason into her selections." Sadie acknowledged that some queens invested more consideration than others. She recalled two years ago when the queen chose her own family members and friends. She'd wanted them all to make good matches as she had, and they did. Could one really blame her for wanting that for herself?

"What would you do if you were queen?" the duke asked.

Sadie would be lying if she said she hadn't thought about it. Any girl growing up in Marrywell imagined herself as a maiden fair and then queen. "I think I would choose the young ladies who need the most help gaining attention. Perhaps those who are shy or quiet."

"Would they be comfortable as maidens fair? You indicated they are the most popular young ladies at the festival."

"If they don't want to be a maiden fair, they wouldn't attend the reception. That's the entire purpose of going. You'll see today that almost everyone there is either an unmarried man seeking a wife, an unmarried lady, or the families—most likely the mothers—of those ladies."

"I assume your mother died," he said. "I'm sorry she can't be here with you. Has she been gone a long time?"

"Since I was eight." Sadie had already been caring for her younger brothers because their mother had been ill. After her death, Sadie had taken on more of her role, but then she'd had the help and support of Mrs. Evans, their housekeeper, until she'd died four years later.

He sent her a sympathetic look. "That is very young. My mother died when I was fourteen."

"I'm sorry to hear that. And since you are a duke, I assume your father is also gone?"

"Yes, he died last autumn. I am still getting used to holding the title, in fact."

She heard a note of unease in his voice and found it surprising. From the moment she'd seen him in the drive, he exuded an air of confidence and vitality, as if he were a man who *did* things instead of watching others. Perhaps she'd made that assessment after he'd caught her and then moved the ladder for her.

"And do you have siblings?" she asked.

"Two younger sisters who are wed. They participated in their own matchmaking festival—in London, we call it the *Season*." He waggled his blond brows.

Sadie laughed. His humor was a bit surprising. "Yes, I've heard of it. Does it have a crowning ceremony, a brewer's field, or a pudding competition?"

He laughed too. "Unfortunately, no. It has presentations to the queen, a never-ending calendar of insipid balls and routs, and, of course, Almack's."

He shuddered. "But one must impress one of the patronesses to be invited there. On second thought, perhaps it's somewhat like wooing your May Queen to become a maiden fair."

"Except you don't have to be a maiden fair to attend the festival," Sadie said. "It sounds as if you don't enjoy the Season."

"It can be tedious, particularly if none of the young ladies on the Marriage Mart strikes your fancy." His gaze moved toward her briefly, but there was something in his eyes that made her feel almost...breathless.

Was he trying to communicate something to her?

Of course not. He was merely being conversational.

Sadie surprised herself by asking, "Is that why you're not wed? No one has struck your fancy?"

"Ah, yes. I think it's fair to say that." He glanced in her direction. "You mentioned a pudding competition. Dare I hope your cook also makes delectable puddings?"

Sadie hoped she hadn't made him uncomfortable with her question. "Indeed, she does. Mrs. Rowell often wins the categories in which she enters, and she's won best overall pudding several times." The pudding competition was one of the few activities Sadie had attended the past four years, along with the Grand Picnic, which really was the most enjoyable event of the festival.

"Please tell me we get to sample them," Lawford said with an endearing enthusiasm.

"I think you may count on being one of the judges. They always seek to choose esteemed members of the community and honored guests. You will surely fall in the latter group."

"I'm beginning to think the wheel coming off

my coach was a rather happy accident indeed." He grinned, his features crinkling and making him look far more approachable and relatable than he had when they'd first met. Sadie wondered how she'd ever judged him austere and arrogant. He was showing himself to be quite amiable and in possession of a warm sense of humor.

They'd arrived in town, and the bustle was nearly overwhelming with traffic and people. Sadie was immediately struck with a pang of anxiety. What if this year was as calamitous as four years ago? She had a sudden urge to return home.

No, this is necessary. Furthermore, the duke's presence may give you an advantage. You're a fool if you don't seize this opportunity.

Since she'd been a fool four years ago, she decided she'd rather avoid being one again.

"This is quite a crush," the duke said. "What am I to do with the gig? We don't have a tiger to watch over it."

"You can park it on Garden Street next to the botanical gardens and there will be boys who keep an eye on the vehicles. The assembly rooms are on the corner of the High Street and Garden Street." She gestured to a street up ahead. "Turn to the left there—that's the High Street."

The crowd was even thicker on the High Street. Sadie saw many faces she knew and even more that she didn't, as the festival drew visitors from a wide radius. The duke drove slowly, navigating the press of vehicles and people with ease.

"You're an excellent driver," she said.

"Thank you. You should see me in my high-perch phaeton." He sent her a sly smile, a subtle variation of the grin he'd flashed earlier. She wondered how many ways he could make her heart skip.

That thought provoked an icy chill to steal over her. The last time she'd fallen prey to a gentleman's charms, she'd found herself in a most embarrassing situation. It could have been much worse, but it was still the most humiliating event of her life. Because of it, she'd avoided courtship and most of all, the matchmaking aspect of this festival.

She couldn't avoid it this year, however, if she intended to have a home and family of her own. She simply needed to keep her wits about her and not be charmed by the silken words of scoundrels.

Snatching her head from the clouds, she took a deep, restorative breath. "The assembly rooms are just up ahead on the corner—on the right. The High Street ends at the garden, so you can turn either left or right to park the gig."

"I'll go left since it's easier." As they turned, he looked toward the botanical gardens. "They look rather extensive. And impeccable, from what I can see."

"They are the pride of Marrywell, after the matchmaking festival, of course. The gardens are where the Grand Picnic takes place, as well as the lawn bowling and badminton, and tonight, the crowning of the May Queen and King. They were chosen at the ball held on the last night of last year's festival, but they aren't given their crowns until this evening."

He maneuvered the gig to the side of the road along the edge of the gardens. "I see. So, if you are named king and queen, you're beholden to return to the next festival. Has anyone not done that?"

"There have been a few occasions, typically involving the birth of a child. I recall hearing about one tragedy, decades ago, when the king was killed in a hunting accident."

"Just like my father," the duke murmured as he climbed out of the gig.

When he came around to help her down, Sadie looked him in the eye. "Is that how he died? I'm sorry, his loss must have been a shock."

The duke took her hand, provoking another flash of awareness that Sadie worked to ignore, and guided her to the ground. "Somewhat. My father had a penchant for doing the most outrageous and potentially dangerous thing possible. He lived to impress and to demonstrate his prowess. There was bound to come a time when the boar—or whatever he pitted himself against—was going to win."

He sounded so matter-of-fact. She wondered if he'd suffered any grief. Perhaps they hadn't been close. She didn't want to pry into his personal matters, so she simply said, "How sad."

The duke looked about, his gaze settling on a boy who was walking near the vehicles that were parked. "Is that one of the lads watching over the horses? I should like to thank him. Or pay him."

"He and the other boys will be paid in whatever food is left from the reception, and their stomachs will be stuffed. But you're welcome to pay them too."

"That's not a bad form of compensation," the duke said, chuckling. "Especially if they get any of Mrs. Rowell's cakes. I'd still like to thank him." Before he could, however, the boy had moved on. "Ah, well, I'm sure I'll see him later." He tucked Sadie's arm around his, and they started toward the assembly rooms.

"People are looking at us." Sadie assumed it was because Lawford was so very tall and good-looking.

"Are they?" He seemed utterly unaware and unbothered.

As soon as they stepped into the assembly rooms, they were greeted by the constable's wife, Mrs. Sneed. In her late forties with a wide, tooth-filled smile, she was one of the primary organizers of the festival. She curtsied to the duke. "Welcome, Your Grace. It is Marrywell's honor to have you here."

It seemed Mrs. Rowell, who'd come earlier to put out her cakes, had shared that Fieldstone was hosting a duke. Sadie was certain Mrs. Sneed had already told as many people as possible. That explained the attention they'd garnered outside.

Mrs. Sneed finally glanced toward Sadie. "Miss Campion, what a surprise to see you here. Given your absence the past few years, I assumed you weren't interested in being a maiden fair."

Sadie clenched her jaw. She wanted to retort with something witty or clever, but words failed her.

"I can think of no better candidate for maiden fair," Lawford said with a touch of his earlier haughtiness. "And I'm afraid she had to attend so she could be my guide." He flashed a thoroughly captivating smile at Sadie, and his demeanor changed, as if he were reserving his true self for her while keeping it from Mrs. Sneed. Sadie doubted that could be true and shook the thought from her head.

"Well, that's splendid of you to pay attention to Miss Campion." Mrs. Sneed somehow managed to make that sound condescending toward Sadie. While still looking at Lawford, she said, "I believe your cook was looking for you, Miss Campion. She is in the refreshment room."

Hoping there was nothing wrong, Sadie turned

to the duke and took her hand from his arm. "Will you excuse me for a few minutes?"

"I'll come with you," he offered.

"That isn't necessary," Mrs. Sneed interjected. "I'd very much like to introduce you to my husband as well as some of Marrywell's leading families, including the mayor and his wife. We are incredibly honored by your presence."

Sadie knew it was hopeless to object. Mrs. Sneed was an immovable force when she wanted something. Besides, Sadie would be gone only a few minutes. Mouthing, *Go,* and smiling at the duke, she turned and hurried to the room where the refreshments would be laid out on tables.

Mrs. Rowell immediately bustled toward her. "Sadie, there you are." Her forehead was creased, and she wrung her hands. "We are somehow missing two of the boxes of cakes, including the ones made special for the queen and king. Bryan's gone back to Fieldstone, but he's on foot. I'm worried he won't be back before the queen leaves."

"She hasn't even arrived yet, so that isn't likely to happen." But Sadie knew how important those cakes were, and not having them would reflect poorly on Mrs. Rowell. Sadie couldn't have that. "I'll take the gig back to Fieldstone to fetch the cakes. I'll pick Bryan up on the way."

"You can't miss the reception," Mrs. Rowell said with genuine concern.

"I won't. We'll be back before too long," Sadie said, hoping that would prove true. "The boxes are in the kitchen?"

"I believe so." The cook put her hand to her forehead in distress. "Things were so very busy with the arrival of the duke. We must have missed them somehow."

Sadie touched the dear woman's arm. "Don't

fret. I'll go now. Will you please tell the duke where I went? I fear he's been intercepted by Mrs. Sneed."

Mrs. Rowell nodded. "Poor man. And thank you, Sadie. You've the kindest heart."

Though Sadie considered bringing the duke with her, she didn't want to waste the time to find him. Besides, he ought to stay and enjoy himself.

Hurrying from a side door, she made her way back to Garden Street, where the gig was parked. Getting it out and through the traffic took longer than she'd anticipated. She worked to tamp down her growing frustration, but as each moment ticked past, she felt her chances for being chosen as a maiden fair slipping away. The queen was likely making her way about the reception now, surveying all the unmarried women and deciding whom she would name in tonight's ceremony. Sadie was missing her opportunity to be seen on the duke's arm.

At last, she arrived at Fieldstone, just as Bryan was entering the drive. He was breathing hard when he climbed into the gig. Together, they found the missing cakes in the kitchen and were soon on their way back to town with Bryan driving this time.

The groom drove straight to the assembly rooms. "You take the box of special cakes in while I park. I'll bring the rest."

"Thank you, Bryan." Sadie climbed down, and in her haste stumbled, stepping on the hem of her gown. She heard fabric tear but had no idea how bad the damage was. Looking over her shoulder, she saw Bryan leaning toward her.

"Are you all right?"

"Yes," she said through gritted teeth. "I've torn my gown, however. Is it bad?"

"Er, I can see your petticoat. Sorry, Sadie."

A dozen curses stormed through her frustrated mind. She couldn't go into the reception like this. "You're going to have to take the cakes inside."

"But you need to go to the reception," Bryan protested.

"Not in my present state." She climbed back into the gig. "You take the cakes. And tell His Grace that I'm waiting outside."

"Where will you park?" Bryan glanced about. "It's quite crowded."

"I'll manage." Unshed tears burned her eyes and throat. Sadie wouldn't cry in front of the groom. Summoning a fake smile, she told him to hurry inside.

He picked up the boxes and dashed toward the side door of the assembly rooms.

Sadie drove on and circled back to the corner. She stared at the assembly rooms with a mix of envy and disappointment. Her last chance to be a maiden fair was gone.

Why had she waited so long to try again? No, why had she let that awful Walter Osborne ruin things for her four years ago so that she hadn't wanted to risk humiliation a second time?

Because it's easier to be at Fieldstone where you manage everything, where you feel capable and comfortable.

An angry tear slid down her cheek. She wiped it away. She wasn't going to let Osborne and that entire horrid experience wreck another matchmaking festival. Sitting in the gig, she took deep breaths and tried to focus on other things, such as how quickly Mavis could repair her gown. It was her best walking dress, and she'd planned to wear it again for the Grand Picnic.

Finally, the May Queen left the assembly rooms

amid much fanfare. Sadie pursed her lips and held herself completely still—like a stone—as she watched more than a dozen unmarried ladies swarming about the entrance. A moment later, the duke emerged.

Straightening, Sadie mentally chided herself. She was not going to wallow in self-pity in front of the duke. So, she wouldn't be a maiden fair. She might yet find a match. Plenty of young women did.

She drove forward and waved to catch the duke's eye. He strode toward her and climbed into the gig.

Lawford's dark gaze regarded her with concern. "The groom told me you had some sort of mishap. What happened?"

She handed him the reins. "I stepped on the back of my gown in an exceedingly clumsy moment. I'm afraid attending the reception with a visible petticoat wasn't possible."

He frowned. "Does this mean you won't be a maiden fair?"

"Yes, but that's fine," she managed to force out.

They drove in silence until they were away from the traffic and heading out of town.

"I am sorry things did not go as planned," he said, still frowning. "I did mention you a few times. You may yet have a chance."

Despite her disappointment, Sadie was flattered and delighted by his support. "That was most kind of you to mention me, but I doubt it."

"May I ask what your ultimate goal is?" He glanced over at her with genuine interest. "Is it to gain popularity or to make a match?"

"One serves the other," she said, feeling self-conscious discussing this matter with the duke, whom she'd just met that very day.

"You want to make a match, then," he concluded. "Very well. Let's make that happen."

Sadie angled her upper body toward him, careful not to move her backside lest she further damage her gown. "You sound so certain, as if all you need to do is wish something into existence."

He shrugged. "If you want something, you should do whatever you can to achieve it."

"I suppose that's relatively easy for a duke."

"With some things, but not everything. I'm saying if you put in the work, you will reap rewards. My father used to say that often, and it was one of the few times I agreed with him."

That answered Sadie's question as to the nature of the duke's relationship with his father. Or at least partly. Now she was curious to know more, but she was more interested in understanding what he was trying to do for her. "How are we going to make a match for me 'happen'?" she asked.

"I'm not entirely certain, but I think if I escort you to the crowning celebration tonight and whatever is happening tomorrow, that would be a good start."

Sadie recalled the attention they'd received earlier when they'd walked to the assembly rooms. It seemed nearly as much as she'd get if she was a maiden fair. Perhaps his plan had merit. "You'd be willing to do that?"

"Aside from the fact that I have nothing better to do this week, I would be delighted to help you. After all, you provided aid to me and my retainers in our hour of need. I would be deeply remiss if I didn't return the kindness."

He felt he owed her. Well, that made sense, she supposed.

He also said he'd be delighted.

Sadie slid him a furtive look. She'd be daft to

refuse his help. Furthermore, why wouldn't she want to be squired about by a handsome duke?

"This is most generous of you," she said. "Thank you."

"Does that mean you accept my offer?" He looked over at her, and the eagerness in his gaze made her heart skip again.

"Yes."

"Excellent. I promise I will do my best to see you betrothed by the end of this festival."

She believed he would try, even if she didn't quite believe the result would happen.

CHAPTER 4

That night, Law rode in the Campions' coach to the crowning ceremony with Miss Campion, her father, and her two younger brothers. Thankfully, Campion had realized it would be too cramped inside, and he'd made the youngest, Richard, ride up top with Bryan, their groom, who was apparently also their coachman.

Law understood why the vehicle hadn't been offered to him. It was positively decrepit. Aside from being ancient, it was in need of refurbishment. He began to wonder if Campion was light on funds. Was his estate not profitable?

Miss Campion was seated across from him next to her father. She wore a pretty but simple ball gown that he'd guess was at least a few years old. That seemed to support the notion that there wasn't enough money, but then again, what need did she have of a new ball gown every year?

Except there was this festival that was clearly of high importance. It seemed reasonable that a young lady who was in want of a husband, such as Miss Campion, might need a new evening gown each year?

There was also the fact that they had no housekeeper or butler and just two maids, one of whom was primarily dedicated to the kitchen.

He really didn't need to be thinking so deeply about her or her family. However, he couldn't seem to help himself. His mind was singularly focused on the alluring young woman, and he'd no idea why.

Perhaps he was simply so eager to avoid his impending betrothal that he'd grasped on to Miss Campion as a welcome distraction. While that made sense, he thought it must be more than just that. In the short time he'd known her, he'd gathered she was engaging, kind, and remarkably capable. She was also stirringly attractive, with those green eyes that assessed everything with a quick cleverness. He'd watched as she'd sprung to aid the cook that afternoon. That she'd left the reception, which had been of vital importance to her, to help someone in her household was a clear demonstration of generosity and loyalty. She was a person Law would want on his side.

He'd felt awful that she'd missed the event and that the reason was because she'd torn her gown. Though she'd tried to hide her disappointment, Law had seen it. He hadn't thought twice about offering his own help. She was also a person who deserved to have others supporting her as she did them.

What Law couldn't yet determine was if her family fit that category. Perhaps tonight he'd find out.

Adam, who was three years younger than Miss Campion, with her same light brown hair, looked to Law. "How did you find the reception, Your Grace?"

"It was quaint." Law saw Miss Campion's brows

arch briefly and realized he probably ought to have used a different word.

"I'm sure it's a much smaller event than you're used to," she said.

"Of course it is," her father agreed. "I imagine His Grace attends lavish balls in London that make our festival look positively rustic."

"What's it like being a duke?" Adam asked.

All three Campions regarded him with interest. Law felt slightly uncomfortable. What was he supposed to say? "I'm not sure I can report with much authority as I've only been a duke about six months."

"You've got six months' experience, then," Adam said eagerly. "What do you do in London? Do you attend a ball every night? Do you ride on Rotten Row every morning? Do you own a phaeton?"

At the last question, Miss Campion hid a smile behind her hand.

"No, I do not attend balls every night, nor do I visit Rotten Row every morning. I do own a phaeton."

Adam grinned. "Brilliant. Do you race?"

"Occasionally." That was one of the few risky activities Law's father had encouraged him to do that he actually enjoyed. Still, he didn't take the risks his father did. The former duke had completely wrecked a phaeton three years ago. That he'd walked away with minor injuries was fortunate, but the fact that the horse had been unscathed was a miracle. Law had taken that poor horse for himself and now used him for his small gig.

"Must be thrilling," Adam said. "How many houses do you own?"

Miss Campion pursed her dark pink, bow-shaped lips, making them look even more kissable than usual. Damn, when had Law started thinking of them as kissable? "Adam, I'm sure His Grace would rather not be badgered with questions."

"I'd like to know too," Campion said with enthusiasm.

A subtle sigh slipped past Miss Campion's lips. It was the sound of surrender, and Law wondered how often she took that stance with her family. He imagined as the sole female amongst so many males, she was challenged and was likely in a constant state of having to assert herself. He also suspected she was victorious more often than not, and that she chose which battles were worth fighting. This one was not—Law would tell them about his bloody houses.

"I own two estates and a house in London, as well as my father's hunting lodge."

"Isn't it your hunting lodge now?" Campion asked, sounding confused.

"I'm not interested in hunting for sport." Law would never think of it as his own and hoped to sell it. "I suppose it's a nice place to visit if one enjoys being cold and damp."

Miss Campion stifled a smile, and Law allowed his lips to lift. He liked making her smile. And now he wanted to turn the tables on these curious Campions. "How large is Fieldstone, Campion?"

"Nine hundred acres," he said proudly. "There are eight tenant farmers, including Esmond and Philip. I'm hoping to purchase a small neighboring estate later this year, which would add another five hundred acres."

If he was going to purchase land, his finances were likely in better shape than Law had surmised. But, if Campion had been saving to make this investment, perhaps that was why there wasn't enough money for other things.

"You must be doing very well," Law said, glancing toward Miss Campion to gauge her opinion on the matter. Her expression revealed nothing.

Campion smoothed his hand down the front of his coat and over his thick middle. "I think so. Still nowhere near being a duke." He laughed.

Thankfully, they'd arrived in town and the coach stopped at one of the main gates to the botanical gardens. Law was eager to get away from their questions. He climbed out first and helped Miss Campion down.

She took his offered arm, and Law escorted her through the gate. The gardens were awash with light from both lanterns and torches. There were several paths, and a dais stood up ahead.

"Is that where the crowning takes place?" Law asked.

"Yes. There will be seven 'thrones' on stage for the maidens fair. They aren't actually thrones, of course, but wrought iron chairs decorated with flowers. There are also thrones for the king and queen, but those are made of brass."

Campion and the two younger sons joined them, and they started along the path toward the dais.

Law could hear Adam telling the younger one, Richard, what he'd missed hearing not being inside the coach. Miss Campion heard them too, for she rolled her eyes and quietly apologized to Law.

"They are most impressed by you," she said. "We've never hosted a peer, let alone a duke."

"What about you? Are you impressed?" Law couldn't tell.

She seemed to assess him, her gaze sweeping

him from head to toe. The thoroughness of her perusal heated his blood. "I suppose I am. You're very tall."

Law laughed. That was his defining quality? "Should I assume you've also never hosted a tall person?"

"That is correct," she said primly but with a bright dash of humor flickering in her eyes.

They encountered Miss Campion's eldest brother, Esmond, and a pretty blonde. Esmond inclined his head. "Your Grace. Allow me to present my wife, Annabelle, Mrs. Campion."

Law bowed to Mrs. Campion. "I'm pleased to make your acquaintance."

The woman curtsied, her hand still gripping her husband's arm as she wavered on her way up. "Your Grace, it is most splendid to meet you." She batted her lashes at him.

Esmond shifted his gaze to his sister. "Sadie, please tell us you're still coming over tomorrow morning to help with the boys. Annabelle is on crown-making duty."

Little pleats dimpled the space between Miss Campion's light brown eyebrows as she looked to the blonde. "I thought I was coming to help you clean the larder."

"I'm hoping you can still do that," Annabelle said. "But my mother needs an extra person to help make the maiden fair crowns in the morning. Unfortunately, my youngest sister, who was to assist her, isn't feeling well."

"I see," Miss Campion said. "Hopefully you won't be gone too long, as I've other chores to complete."

"You can always take the boys back to Fieldstone with you," Annabelle suggested with a shrug.

Miss Campion blinked at her.

"I'm sure their grandpapa would be happy to play with them," Annabelle added with a glance toward Campion.

"Not tomorrow," Campion said loudly. "I've a meeting with Rowell."

"It will be fine," Miss Campion assured everyone.

"The whole family's here!" A gentleman who was presumably the fourth Campion son for he bore quite a resemblance to their father, approached with a dark-haired woman.

"Philip, have you met the duke?" Esmond asked.

"Not yet." Philip bowed to Law. "This is my wife, Mrs. Janet Campion."

Law inclined his head. "How nice to meet you."

Philip looked at where Miss Campion clutched Law's arm. "Are you escorting our Sadie?"

"Not really," Miss Campion answered quickly. "I'm acting as his guide since he is unfamiliar with the festival." She looked up at Law. "In fact, let me show you the refreshment area."

Before anyone could respond, she'd tugged him around and pulled him along the path at a very fast walk.

"Are we in a hurry?" he asked.

"Yes. To get away from my family." She glanced up at him. "Sorry, that isn't very kind of me to say."

"On the contrary, it's more than kind. You demonstrate a remarkable level of patience and generosity. I was thinking in the coach that it must be difficult for you to manage four brothers, your father, and a household. It seems I must also add two brothers' families to that as well. Or should I not presume that you also help Philip?"

A sheepish look swept her features. "You've sorted that out quickly. I *have* been helping Janet with managing her household. She's new to the task. And yes, it is difficult. I'm…I'm surprised you noticed."

"Why, because I'm a duke?"

"No, because you're a man."

"That is true, and your point is well taken." They slowed their pace, and Law decided to satisfy his curiosity. "Why doesn't your sister-in-law just take her sons with her to make crowns? And why does she even need to make crowns? Won't the maidens have them already if they're to be crowned tonight?"

"They're made of flowers, and the queen and maidens get new ones every day. Annabelle's mother is in charge of them, so it makes sense that she would enlist her help, though she hadn't planned to since she has her hands full with two children this year. She could take the boys, but then she wouldn't actually be much help."

"It sounds as if you'll have *your* hands full," he said with a hint of annoyance. It appeared Miss Campion's family took advantage of her. "And she still expects you to clean her larder."

"She can expect all she likes, but I can't see that happening if I'm watching over the boys. The whole reason I'd agreed to help her was because it would be easier to complete the chore with two of us managing both that and the children."

He heard that she was irritated too. Good, she should be.

"I must apologize for my father's and brother's behavior in the coach. They were rather impertinent with their questions." A smile teased her kissable lips—hell, could he not think of them any other way? "I appreciated you asking my father about Fieldstone, but I doubt he realized the irony."

Law doubted it too, but was glad she'd enjoyed

the turnabout. "I confess I was curious too. I wondered if your family was experiencing financial hardship."

She swung her head toward him. "You did?"

"Your lack of sufficient help with the household and…a few other things indicated that might be the case."

She nodded. "With one look at the coach, you could easily surmise that we're destitute. Thankfully, we are not. My father is just very frugal. He puts a great deal of money back into the estate. He's also been saving for the purchase of the neighboring land."

"He shouldn't allow his household to suffer."

Miss Campion nodded. "My father has ideas, but doesn't necessarily possess the skills to execute them. Thankfully, he has me and Rowell—he's the land manager."

"And married to the cook, I gather?" Since they shared the same surname, though he supposed they could be siblings.

"Yes. You'll have to meet him. He's not as friendly as Mrs. Rowell, but he can tell you anything you'd like to know about farming or animal husbandry."

"I actually wouldn't mind speaking to him about sheep, if he has the time."

"He'd love to talk with you—just know that you may be with him for some time. He can be loquacious about his work."

Law realized they were on a path that circled around toward the dais. He didn't see refreshments anywhere. "We aren't going to the refreshment area, are we?"

"I'm afraid not. We can, if you like, but the ceremony will begin soon. Oh, look, the mayor is preparing to speak."

They found a place to stand near the dais. She clutched his arm tightly, and Law wondered if she was nervous. "Is there any chance you could be chosen as a maiden fair?" he asked.

"The slightest one, perhaps, since you mentioned me. However, I don't expect it."

But she wanted it. Law wished he could turn back the clock and be the one to fetch the forgotten cakes. "I would have returned to Fieldstone for you," he said softly. "You should have stayed at the reception."

She stared at him, her eyes glittering like emeralds, but if she planned to respond, she was prevented from doing so by the mayor speaking.

A round-faced, dark-eyed man in his sixties, he welcomed everyone to the festival and provided some history about when and why it was founded. None of it sounded verifiable, but it made a nice story. Then he introduced the May King and Queen—Mr. and Mrs. Martinscroft. Martinscroft was the heir to Baron Tippenworth, whom Law did not know.

The orchestra played an interval of music as the mayor, Mr. Armstrong, placed an elaborate floral crown atop the queen's head and a less…flowery version on the king. There was much applause, and the mayor declared the festival officially begun. This included an announcement that the labyrinth was now open.

"There's a labyrinth?" he whispered to Miss Campion. "I'd like to see that. Perhaps you can show me after the ceremony."

"There will be dancing immediately following the ceremony," she said, her gaze fixed on the dais.

The queen came forward to read the names of the seven maidens fair. As each one was called, Miss Campion stiffened. Then she relaxed only to tense again. As the final name was revealed, he felt her sag and wondered if she might be relieved. But that didn't make sense since he knew she'd wanted to be a maiden fair.

"I'm glad that's over," she said with a bright smile. "They will start the dancing now."

"I believe the queen has made a massive oversight," Law said. "None of those maidens on the dais compares to you."

She cocked her head. "How can you know that? You just met me this morning."

"You've made a very favorable impression." Law also didn't like losing, which he blamed on his father. Nothing was more important than being recognized as the best. And yes, for whatever reason, he liked Miss Campion and wanted her to win. More accurately, he wanted her to have what she wanted, what she deserved when she worked so hard for everyone else around her.

"It's all right, truly," she assured him.

He was going to say there was always next year, but he'd promised he would do his best to see her betrothed by the end of the week. This was one time he absolutely *couldn't* lose.

"Come, we need to move out of the way, as this is where people will dance."

He realized the ground had been leveled to form a dance floor and was devoid of grass or plants. Escorting her back to the path, he asked, "What are you looking for in a husband?"

"Why do you want to know?"

"I'm committed to seeing you betrothed, Miss Campion. It would help me to know what sort of gentleman you desire." He sensed a ripple moving through the woman beside him. Perhaps he should have used a different word from "desire." Or perhaps the ripple had come from him.

"I suppose I would like to marry a man who is strong and capable, and who is also clever and kind." Those were words Law would have used to describe her. "Mostly, I want my own household to run, my own family." She spoke softly and with great longing.

"Then you shall have it," he said with confidence. There were a great many gentlemen here looking for a bride. Surely one of them would meet her needs. No, her potential husband had to do better than that—he needed to capture her heart. Nothing less would do for Miss Campion.

"Would you care to dance with me, Miss Campion?" he asked.

She looked into his eyes and smiled. "I would, thank you."

He led her toward where the maidens had started the dancing a few minutes ago. By the end of the night, she'd have danced with at least a handful of suitors, and tomorrow, she'd dance with even more. At the Grand Picnic, she'd be the most sought-after woman at the festival—never mind the maidens—and she'd have her pick of husbands.

Though he'd only just met her, Law felt certain that was what she deserved.

CHAPTER 5

Stifling a yawn, Sadie applied more pressure to the crust she was rolling out on the worktable in the kitchen. She was helping to make several pies to have on hand to feed everyone. Mrs. Rowell was always busy during the festival baking cakes for the welcome reception and then making a variety of puddings for the pudding competition. This year was even busier since they had three additional members in their household.

"You may need a quick nap this afternoon," Mrs. Rowell said with a chuckle.

Sadie hadn't managed to keep from yawning after all. "I am not usually up as late as I was last night. And you know I don't nap."

"I do know that. You barely even sit down. What time did you return from the festival?"

"After midnight." Then, she'd been up early to complete some chores before going to Esmond's to watch the boys so Annabelle could make crowns. As expected, Sadie hadn't accomplished much with cleaning the larder, but she'd enjoyed the time with her nephews.

"I hope you had a nice evening with the duke.

Did he ask you to dance?" the cook asked with a sly smile.

"He did, in fact." After that first dance, she'd danced with several other gentlemen. Some of her partners were men she knew from Marrywell, such as her old friend Phineas Radford, whose family owned and cared for the botanical gardens, but most were gentlemen she'd never met who had come from out of town. She'd felt a trifle uncomfortable with them as she recalled her foolishness that first year with Walter Osborne. He'd been from Bath, and he'd completely enthralled her with his good looks and easy charm.

But she needed to overcome her reticence if she wanted to find a husband. She'd learned from her mistake and wouldn't be so gullible this time.

Perhaps one of the men from Marrywell would suffice. Except she'd known a few of them for so long that considering them as potential husbands seemed odd.

It was far too soon to make any judgments. There were many more days of festival left, and with the duke's help, she might indeed receive an offer of marriage.

She wondered what he might be doing to assist her—besides promenading and dancing with her. Was he complimenting her to other gentlemen? Or prompting them to invite her to dance? Whatever he was doing, she'd never felt so…seen. It was at once wonderful and disconcerting. She was much more used to lingering in the background, such as helping to set up the welcome reception or the pudding competition, and making sure things went smoothly.

"Is something wrong with the dough?" Mrs. Rowell asked.

Sadie blinked. She'd stopped rolling as she'd become lost in her thoughts. "Not at all. Just woolgathering. So many things to do before I attend the festival this evening."

"You aren't going this afternoon?"

"No, I've too much to do," Sadie's long list included making entries in the household account book, sweeping the downstairs, and replacing candles.

"Bryan and Gwen plan to attend the lawn bowling competition," Mrs. Rowell said.

Sadie allowed their employees to attend as many festival events as possible, especially the young unmarried ones. "Mavis isn't going with them?"

"I believe she will be reading to Mr. Holden," Mrs. Rowell said with a pointed look.

"Oh? How fascinating." Sadie smiled as she wondered what might be blossoming between her maid and the duke's coachman. Then her smile faded. What if Mavis fell in love and they got married? She'd leave Fieldstone, and Sadie would have even more to do.

They'd hire another maid, of course, but honestly, they needed a housekeeper. Having Lawford point that out to her was both embarrassing and provoking. She hadn't broached the subject with her father in a long time. When she thought about it, she hadn't mentioned it in four years, not since the incident with Walter Osborne when Sadie had subsequently hidden herself away at Fieldstone.

She winced inwardly. Was that really what she'd been doing?

It seemed so. But not any longer. This was the year she'd find her way. She'd get married and have a household of her very own.

Fieldstone and her family would just have to learn to manage without her.

~

Law had hoped to break his fast with Miss Campion that morning, but he hadn't risen early enough—and he hadn't slept late. Apparently, she awakened with the birds, which he should have realized. However, he'd been tired after yesterday's accident. Indeed, he could hardly believe he'd been able to stay upright as late as he had last night.

Today, his body was sore in odd places. After missing Miss Campion for breakfast, he'd submitted to a lengthy toilet with Yates, who'd insisted on applying some relaxing concoction to his face that had turned his skin red. Yates had apologized profusely before retreating, and Law had decided to go back to sleep in the hope that he'd wake up looking like himself. While he felt much restored this afternoon, his face was, regrettably, still the color of a strawberry.

In need of something to do, he made his way to the stables to see how his coach was coming along with its repair. Or *if* it was even coming along. Holden was still recuperating today and would not be available to assist them, even though he would only be providing verbal help. Law had been explicit in telling the coachman that he must not overexert himself. The last thing Holden wanted was to worsen his injury. Furthermore, it seemed the housemaid was spending an inordinate amount of time visiting and caring for him. Yates had complained about the situation, and Law had told him to stop being such a prig.

As Law approached the door to the stables, he heard a...discussion going on inside.

"It doesn't go on like that!" one male voice yelled.

"As if you know!" another snapped.

Steeling himself for quarreling brothers, Law stepped into the cool interior of the stone building.

"Your Grace, are you here to see the coach?" Richard asked. A lad of seventeen with dark blond hair and inquisitive hazel eyes, he was taller than his older brothers and possessed a more slender build, as if he hadn't yet filled into his manhood.

"Indeed I am." Law moved into the interior of the barn where the vehicle was braced on a wooden contraption to hold it up so the wheel could be reattached. "I came to see how the repair is progressing."

Law noted that all four brothers were present. Last night, Miss Campion had laughingly described them, in order of birth, as: Esmond, the handsome one; Philip, the witty one; Adam, the talkative one; and Richard, the clever one.

The other three Campion brothers stopped what they were doing and turned to face Law. "Your Grace," they said, nearly in unison, sounding almost as if they'd been caught behaving naughtily. He imagined the four of them looking at their sister guiltily and saying her name in the same tone, because Law was certain she must have caught them misbehaving on more than one occasion.

Philip stared at Law, his mouth gaping, "What happened to your face?"

"My valet misapplied something."

Adam moved closer to Law, his gaze riveted to Law's face. "Does it hurt?"

"No. It just looks like I'm burning in hell." Too

late, Law recalled he was speaking to Marrywell's new curate.

Adam smirked, his hazel eyes gleaming with humor. "Or you're the devil himself."

Law had been accused of many things, but never that. He would have reserved that description for his father, who in turn would have delighted in it. Law could hear his low, deep laugh now. He'd say it was better to be in control of something, even if it was hell.

Philip laughed and glanced toward the oldest brother. "You look like Esmond that time he worked all day with his shirt off in the summer. He was red as a hot coal."

Esmond grimaced. "That was very painful. Glad your face doesn't hurt, Your Grace. Will you be able to escort Sadie to the festival tonight?"

"Certainly." Law was curious if they were always this interested in their sister's activities. However, he decided the likeliest outcome from learning that would be annoyance with them and their lack of care for their sister.

Law had participated in his sisters' introductions to Society and had provided support in their securing good marriages. He'd attended events with them, danced with them, introduced them to potential husbands. Indeed, his youngest sister had married one of his friends from Oxford.

"Who'd care to apprise me on the repair of my coach?" Law asked, looking from brother to brother.

"You didn't have to come all this way," Esmond said, seeming a little uneasy. "We could have told you about it later."

"It's a three-minute walk." Law stepped closer to the coach. "Besides, I wanted to see it for myself. Have you made much progress?" He couldn't tell.

Philip put his hands on his hips as he surveyed the vehicle. "Some."

The lack of details was perhaps telling, but since Law wasn't in any hurry to leave, he didn't see the point in pressing for them. He also saw no benefit in offering to help. Unless he wanted to see if they actually knew what they were doing. He wasn't too worried. Holden would probably be up and about tomorrow and could make sure the repair was completed properly.

"Are you courting Sadie?" Esmond asked, as if Law hadn't completely changed the subject.

Philip turned toward him. "We think you should. She'd make you a fine duchess."

"Have you tried playing matchmaker with her before?" Law asked.

The brothers exchanged looks. It was Richard who answered. "No, but she hasn't been very interest—"

"We don't like to meddle in her business," Esmond said, tossing a glower at Richard. "You seemed to enjoy yourselves last night. Can't fault us for wanting to see our sister happy."

"No, I cannot. I hope that is what you are truly after." Because she'd also danced with other gentlemen and seemed to enjoy her time with them too. Were they also asking those men about potential courtship?

Esmond stuck out his chin. "What else would we want?"

"If you truly cared about your sister, you would have ensured that she was able to stay at the reception yesterday so that she could meet the May Queen instead of her having to be the one to return here to fetch forgotten cakes. You should also ensure she's able to attend the festival instead of expecting her to help with your chores when she seems to have more than enough of her own." Law wanted to see Miss Campion have a day, even a month, hell, an entire lifetime without hard work.

They were silent a moment, but then Richard spoke. "I would have gone to get the cakes if I'd—"

"You don't know Sadie," Esmond said to Law with indignation. "She has a mind of her own. If she doesn't want to do something, she doesn't do it. Anyway, she *likes* working."

"That doesn't mean she needs to do it so much. Or that she wouldn't rather attend a once-a-year event where she might find a husband—an endeavor that you claim to support." Law exhaled before regarding them with an icy stare. "Perhaps you should find ways to lessen her burden."

"I don't even live in the house with her," Esmond said defensively.

Philip snorted. "No, but she brings things to your cottage all the time, and she often helps with the boys."

"She's their aunt!" Esmond turned on his brother, putting one fist on his hip. "She brings things to you and Janet too. Didn't she mend your shirt last week because Janet doesn't like mending?"

"We're newlyweds. Sadie's just being kind."

"She's always kind," Richard muttered, sounding exasperated, not that Law blamed him. His brothers seemed to like to talk over him. "We *could* ensure she has time for leisurely pursuits."

The brothers fell silent, and Law wondered how often that happened.

"It's so quiet in here." Miss Campion walked into the stables looking lovely despite the drab brown of her work dress. Her light brown hair was pinned up, but a few errant strands grazed her temples and neck. She narrowed her eyes at her brothers. "What are you plotting?"

Law noted that she didn't seem to include him in that question, but would answer anyway. "I came to check on my coach. As you can see, they haven't accomplished much."

Miss Campion's eyes rounded as she fixed on Law's face. "What happened?"

"My valet applied something that has turned my skin an unfortunate color."

She stepped toward him, lifting her hand as if she might touch him. His body quivered with anticipation. But she quickly dropped her hand back to her side. "Does it hurt?" she asked.

"Not at all. It's fine."

"Mrs. Rowell might have something that will help. We can go ask her when you're finished here." She looked at Esmond. "Has Jarvis been able to help you?"

"He needed to tend one of his horses." Esmond lifted a burly shoulder. "We can manage without him."

Miss Campion tipped her head to the side, her lips pursing as if she wasn't sure she believed that. She pivoted toward Law. "I'm so sorry, Your Grace. You must think us inept."

"Not at all." He would never include her in such a description. "I'm confident it will be repaired in due time—and done well." Particularly when Holden was here to supervise. Offering Miss Campion his arm, he said, "May I escort you back to the house?"

"You may. I need to complete the task you, ah, interrupted yesterday with your arrival, but I can do that after we see Mrs. Rowell."

Law arched a brow at her. "You're going to

finish cleaning the front door by yourself? On a ladder?"

"I could help," Richard said, stepping toward her.

Law definitely liked Richard best. "That's excellent of you to offer. However, I think I should be the one to provide assistance since it was me who prevented her from completing it yesterday."

Richard's brow furrowed. "But I can—"

Esmond scooted toward his youngest brother and jabbed an elbow into his side, cutting him off. "We need you here."

Miss Campion smiled at Richard. "Thank you. I appreciate you wanting to help."

"I will with anything, whenever I'm here and not at school. Just ask."

"I'll remember that." She took Law's arm, and they left the stables. When they were several paces away, she glanced back over her shoulder. "Were they being awful?"

"No. Richard seems pleasant."

"He is. They all are, mostly. But Richard is the most sensitive. Perhaps I should also have called him the kindhearted one when I was describing them to you last night."

"We don't need to see Mrs. Rowell first," Law said. "In fact, 'we' don't need to visit her at all. I am perfectly capable of seeking her help."

Miss Campion snapped her gaze to his. "I didn't mean to imply you weren't."

"I didn't take it that way. I suppose I'm trying to say that you needn't do everything. I imagine you are busy given that you had to spend time at your brother's cottage this morning. You'll want to take time to prepare for this evening's endeavors in husband hunting."

Laughing, she said, "I'm not sure I like how that sounds."

"It's accurate, however."

"I'd prefer to think of it as happiness hunting. Finding just a husband isn't enough."

Law stared at her as they walked, amazed at how deeply she touched him. Happiness hunting was something he'd never, ever considered, and yet when he looked back at his own wife seeking, he realized that was why he hadn't wed. He hadn't yet met a woman who made him feel…happy. "That's a wonderful sentiment."

They fell into silence for a moment, and Law decided this was a good time to ask about moving Yates to a new room. "I hate to add to your burdens, but I wonder if Yates could move to another room. He can be…stringent, and Holden needs his rest."

"Actually, Mavis is already moving him. 'Stringent' was not the word she used, but she said it was necessary for Holden's state of mind that the two be separated."

Law grimaced. "I'm sorry to cause you trouble."

"It's no trouble to me—Mavis is taking care of it and happily so. I think she's taken a liking to your coachman."

"Indeed?" Law wondered if the matchmaking festival cast a spell over everyone in the vicinity. Was that why he was more drawn to Miss Campion than he'd ever been to a woman?

She looked up at his face, her nose wrinkling slightly. "Are you sure it doesn't hurt?"

He touched his cheek. "Yes. But I'm confident it makes me look ridiculous, so perhaps my vanity is a trifle wounded."

"You don't look ridiculous at all," she said quickly.

"If you're going to lie, make it believable," he said, smiling.

She chuckled. "That sounds like advice you've received. All right, perhaps you appear a *trifle* absurd."

"My father was a font of advice." Except it was typically shared more as a directive than something Law could take or leave.

"How helpful."

Law laughed. Loudly.

"Why is that amusing?"

"Because his advice was nearly always unsolicited. Nor has the bulk of it proved very helpful."

"Ah," she said with understanding. "Thankfully, I don't have to deal with much of that. I am mostly left to my own devices."

"Is that a good thing?"

"Usually, yes." The breeze blew the loose strands of her hair, and Law's finger itched to tuck one behind her ear. Then he'd drag his fingertip down the outer rim. And down farther, to her neck, then all the way to the edge of her bodice.

What on earth was he thinking?

That she was beautiful, clever, and in need of someone who would make her the center of their world.

He needed to distract himself from such pointless thoughts. His goal was to find her a husband who would make her happy, and he was not that man. And it wasn't just the fact that he might have to wed Lady Frederica. Why would a competent, clever woman such as Miss Campion, who simply wanted her own household to manage, want to saddle herself with the complication of becoming a duchess?

They neared the front door, and Miss Campion

took her hand from his arm. "I moved the ladder out of the way. Let me fetch it."

As she started striding toward a pair of trees, he caught up to her. "I'll get it," he said. "Why did you move it if you weren't finished?"

"I couldn't just leave it there to look terrible, not with you coming and going to the festival. And I only put the broom on the porch before walking to the stables to check on your coach."

They reached the trees, and he picked up the ladder. "You were concerned about how this would look to *me?*" *And* she'd gone to check on his coach.

She lifted a shoulder as they went back toward the door. "I realize Fieldstone is far beneath your typical lodging or domicile. I can't help feeling somewhat self-conscious about that." Color flagged her cheeks, and he hated that she was embarrassed.

"Fieldstone is charming, and I'm incredibly impressed with how well it's run with so few retainers. You are to be commended. All day, every day."

"You are extremely complimentary. I would ask you to stop, but I confess it's lovely to hear." She gave him a sheepish smile that crinkled her features in the most adorable fashion. He just wanted to stare because he simply couldn't get enough of her.

She grabbed the broom from beside the door as he set the ladder. "How are you planning to assist me?"

Taking the broom from her, he met her gaze. "I am going to climb up there and finish the job while you watch from the comfort of the ground. Or you could go about your other duties, if you prefer."

"And leave you alone without help or supervision?" She shook her head firmly as a smile danced upon her eminently kissable lips. "Not a chance, Your Grace."

"Law," he said. "I think, given our alliance in your happiness hunting, that you must call me Law."

"I couldn't. At least, not when others are around."

He shrugged. "Do as you like, but it would please me to hear my name on your lips." His choice of words was unintentionally provocative. At least to him. Was it to her?

He could only hope.

And why was that? What on earth would he do with a mutual attraction with Miss Campion? The thought sent a spike of desire straight through him. Miss Campion was beautiful, intelligent, and Law enjoyed her company more than any woman he'd met.

As heat flooded his body, he was grateful that his face was already red. Otherwise, she would have seen the flush coming over him as he worked to tamp down his sudden, rampant lust.

"All right, Law. You may call me Sadie when we are alone."

He would also call her Sadie in his dreams, for he was bound to have them about her. "I'm going up now."

As he climbed the ladder, she asked, "Have you ever knocked down cobwebs before?"

"Never. I once tried to knock a kite out of a tree, but I doubt this is quite the same."

Sadie laughed. "This is probably easier. Were you successful? With the kite, I mean."

"Eventually. However, I ended up climbing higher into the tree to get it loose, and then I was too scared to make my way down. One of the grooms had to fetch me. After that, my father made me practice climbing up and down trees every day until I was nimble as a cat."

"I can't decide if that's horrible."

Law batted at the cobwebs. "At the time, I thought it was cruel because I was so frightened. However, after the first day, my mother came to watch. She told me it was good to conquer fear. It got easier after that."

"Your mother sounds lovely."

"She was. I miss her sometimes." He also missed the man his father had been before she'd died. Nearly all the cobwebs were gone, but there was one corner he couldn't quite reach. Bracing his hand on the stone in front of him, he reached his other arm out as far as possible, extending his hand until pain shot up his wrist.

"Careful!" Sadie called, as if she realized he was almost to the point of reaching too far. "We can move the ladder."

They probably ought to, but he heard his father's voice telling him not to be a coward, that if he just tried a little harder, he could do it...

Law relaxed his arm and pulled the broom back before climbing down. "Yes, let's move it."

Stepping off the last rung, he turned and was surprised to find her standing very close. So close that he could see small gold rims in her eyes separating the pupils from the irises. His heart picked up speed, and his lungs suddenly had to work harder.

"I didn't think you were going to come down," she said softly. "You had me worried there for a moment."

"I didn't mean to cause you distress. I confess to having an internal battle, but ultimately decided safety should win out."

Her lips—those utterly, deliciously kissable lips—turned up. "I'm glad."

Law was so focused on her mouth that he

nearly forgot where he was and what he was doing. "I'll just move this and finish up." He forced himself to turn back and move the ladder.

He climbed up and cleared out the rest of the cobwebs, his body raging with an almost desperate desire. Was there any chance she might feel the same?

Now was not the time to ask. Hell, there would never be a time to ask. He needed to keep his wits about him before he did something he would regret.

Except he was fairly certain he'd never regret anything that happened between himself and Sadie.

Returning to the ground, he handed her the broom. "All clean."

"Too bad we can't hire you," she said, her eyes sparkling with mirth. "Once I'm married, Fieldstone will need more help."

"I'm not sure I'd want to work here without you."

"Oh. Well. I can't imagine you'd want to work here at all." She laughed, but it had a nervous, uncertain quality to it.

He feared he'd overstepped. "Where does the ladder go?" he asked, adopting a businesslike tone.

"In the stables."

She'd carried it from there yesterday? Or had someone carried it for her? He wasn't sure what was worse, but decided it was the latter, for then whoever had transported it had allowed her to complete the risky task alone.

The sooner he helped Sadie find a husband, the sooner she could start her life away from Fieldstone. He'd make sure the gentleman was thoughtful and considerate, and that he understood Sadie's exceptional character.

As he picked up the ladder and started to turn, she put her hand on his arm. The touch was gentle and brief, but the repercussions traveled through his entire body.

"Thank you, Law. I never would have imagined a duke could be so helpful and kind."

"It's my pleasure to be of assistance to you." He inclined his head, then left her presence, glad for the distance he was putting between them.

If he wasn't careful, he was going to forget that he was helping her to find a man who wasn't him.

CHAPTER 6

As Sadie entered the botanical gardens that evening on Law's arm, she glanced over at his face. It had not yet regained its normal shade, but the color had faded to pale pink at least. She'd said he didn't have to accompany her, but he'd insisted—unless she preferred not to be seen with him. Sadie had rolled her eyes in response and said she would've gone with him when his face was still red.

"Good evening, Your Grace, Miss Campion!" Mrs. Sneed hurried toward them, one of her close friends, Mrs. Whimple, at her hip. Mrs. Sneed's gaze swept over Sadie, her nose wrinkling briefly as if she found fault with Sadie's rather plain ball gown. Or perhaps it was with the thick shawl Sadie had draped around her shoulders because it was somewhat cold this evening.

"You've arrived together again!" Mrs. Sneed said. "But I suppose that's to be expected since His Grace is lodging at Fieldstone." She turned her expectant gaze on the duke. "If you'd prefer to be in town, you could always stay with us." She smiled broadly, revealing her mostly straight teeth.

"Oh, yes." Mrs. Whimple, a woman in her fifties with wide brown eyes and white hair, nodded.

"That's very generous of you, Mrs. Sneed, but I'm quite comfortable at Fieldstone. Besides, my coach is being repaired there."

Sadie was fairly certain her brothers were dallying on purpose, probably at her father's behest in order to ensure the duke remained at Fieldstone. She ought to speak with Jarvis personally and ask if he could ensure the coach was fixed with due haste—and skill. While she hated to bother him in his retirement, she also knew he'd do anything she asked. Indeed, if he later learned that she *hadn't* come to him with her concerns, he might take offense. She'd talk to him first thing tomorrow.

Mrs. Sneed pushed her lips into a brief pout. "Well, if you change your mind, you've only to let me know. I do hope the Campions are taking proper care of you." The insinuation in her tone was that they were not.

"I've no complaints," the duke said merrily.

"Should we take our seats?" Sadie asked, even though there was probably a quarter hour until the performances were due to start. She looked up at the duke, hoping he would catch her hint.

"Let's." Law smiled quickly and somewhat unenthusiastically at the ladies. "Have a nice evening." He inclined his head, and he and Sadie continued walking along the path.

Sadie noted he was walking rather quickly. She had to work to keep up with him and his longer legs. "We don't need to hurry. We actually have plenty of time."

"I'm aware of that. I just wanted to put some distance between us and Mrs. Sneed. I don't think I care for her."

"She's harmless. During the festival, she puts on

a cavalier attitude with people who are not from Marrywell. The higher your station, the haughtier she'll behave."

"How very London of her."

Sadie laughed. "Is that how it is in the *ton*?" She gave the word her best French pronunciation. Though she'd studied the language, she'd never mastered it.

"Most definitely." His gaze moved to the side where their path was about to intersect with another. "Here come your father and one of your brothers."

Indeed, her father and Adam were striding right for them, as if they were on a mission. "Sadie! Your Grace!"

"How lovely you look this evening," her father said with a doting smile. He could be difficult to live with, but Sadie never doubted his love for her. "I see you're wearing your mother's citrine necklace. It sparkles quite nicely on you."

"Thank you, Papa." She felt a surge of love for him, but also for her mother. Sadie wished she could be here now.

Her father pivoted to the duke. "How are you finding our festival, Your Grace?"

"It's quite something. Honestly, these events would rival many in London. I'm looking forward to tonight's performances. I do enjoy musicales and the theatre."

"I haven't ever been to the theatre," Sadie said rather wistfully. She'd never imagined visiting London, but the more the duke mentioned it, the more her curiosity grew. A stiff breeze blew into them, and Sadie pressed herself against the duke's side as she shivered.

"This isn't the best weather," Adam observed,

glancing up at the dark sky. A thick cover of clouds completely obliterated the stars and moon.

Sadie followed his gaze and was rewarded with a raindrop on her cheek. "Oh dear, that's rain."

"Just a drop or two," her father said with a wave of his hand.

The rain began to fall steadily in large, dampening drops. People began to rush for the gates leading out of the park.

Pulling her shawl up over her bare head, Sadie looked to the duke. "If we try to leave, we'll be trapped in the crush. There's a folly down that path." She gestured to where her father and brother had come from. "We could take cover there."

"Capital idea, Sadie." Her father was already turning in that direction, as was Adam.

"No, no, don't have your daughter precede you," the duke muttered with sarcastic heat.

"They don't mean any harm," Sadie said, feeling as though she must defend her family.

"They certainly don't mean any aid either. Come, I'll get you to the folly." Law swept her into his arms.

She gasped as he began to walk very quickly after her father and brother. "You can't carry me."

"It seems I can." He passed them, but was moving quickly enough that she didn't hear or see their reactions. "I see the folly." Impossibly, he started to run.

Sadie clutched at his coat and pressed herself against him, as if that might help. Not that he needed any help.

They arrived at the folly, an octagonal structure with, thankfully, a roof. Some of the follies in the gardens were faux ruins, but this wasn't one of them.

Law set her down and shook out his shoulders. "All right?"

Shivering again, Sadie pulled her now very damp shawl back down around her shoulders. "Good enough. Hopefully, the rain will stop."

Though many people had gone directly for the gates, a very large number had dashed to this folly. As more and more entered, she and Law moved farther back into the structure. There were so many people that Sadie didn't see whether her father and brother had come in. She tried to find them and, in that moment or two, was separated from Law.

Glancing about, she couldn't see him among the crowd. She stood on her toes to no avail.

"Miss Campion, how pleasing to find you here." The male voice came from her left.

Sadie turned to see a man she'd met and danced with last night, Mr. Percival Finch. "Good evening, Mr. Finch. Or perhaps not, since I think the musicale is quite ruined," she added with a smile. "I wonder if they'll simply postpone it until tomorrow."

"But aren't there other events tomorrow?" Mr. Finch asked.

She recalled that it was his first time at the festival. "Yes, but it will be simple enough to delay the dancing until after the performances. I should hate for the singers and dancers and musicians to not be able to perform."

"Mmm, yes, a shame indeed." His gaze roved over her, pausing briefly at her chest. "Your shawl is wet. Shall I shake it out for you?"

Sadie reasoned that it would probably be more useful if it weren't so wet. "Thank you, that would be very kind."

She swept it carefully from her shoulders and

handed it to him. His gaze again locked on her bodice as he halfheartedly shook her shawl.

"Careful!" someone said, and Sadie realized Mr. Finch was sending water from her shawl onto other people. While still staring at her overly large chest.

Glancing down, she saw that her dress was also damp, and the fabric was clinging to her in a bawdy fashion, as if her breasts needed any help drawing attention. Realizing what Mr. Finch was about, she folded her arms across her chest.

Law was suddenly there, ripping Sadie's shawl from Mr. Finch's grip. The duke towered over the man, his eyes narrowed and his lip curling. "If you don't stop staring, I'll make sure every unmarried female at the festival knows what a despicable bounder you are." He clipped the words out in a harsh, icy tone. "And that is after I plant my fist in your face."

Mr. Finch opened and closed his mouth like a fish flopping on the bank of a stream. Without a word, he rushed through the crowded throng as if the folly were on fire.

Sadie realized several people around them had overheard what Law said. They were watching Sadie and him with keen interest.

"I'm sorry we were separated." Law's demeanor had changed completely, softening as he put the shawl back around her shoulders, careful to ensure the drier side was next to her. Still, the garment wasn't going to provide much help in its current condition.

Sadie began to shake with cold. "Thank you for intervening. I thought he was trying to help."

"He *was* helping—himself." The duke frowned. "Damn, you're far too cold. Here." He shrugged out of his coat and replaced the shawl with it. Instantly,

Sadie was enveloped in his sandalwood scent, reminding her of when he'd caught her in his arms the day before. Had that only been yesterday?

"It's wet on the outside, but it's thicker than your shawl and will keep you warm," he said. "I need to get you home."

Looking out at the gardens, Sadie was surprised to see they were nearly empty. People had found their way out or into this folly or perhaps others. The rain, however, was still falling steadily. "If we leave now, we'll get drenched. I think we have to wait until the rain at least slows." She faced him, grateful for his coat but worried that he wasn't wearing it. "You'll be cold. If you aren't already."

"It's fine. I have this lovely shawl to keep me warm." He draped it around his shoulders with a flirtatious smile. "As an extra benefit, it smells like you."

Did he find her scent as arousing as she found his? Wait, *arousing*?

Yes. She was reminded of the stolen kisses she'd shared at her first festival, when she'd been foolish enough to think the first man who paid her interest would also marry her. Then she'd learned that kissing in the labyrinth was a rite of passage in Marrywell. All the girls did it.

But all the girls did not attend the festival with a duke who caused their heart to race and said things that made them feel singularly...wonderful.

Except none of this was real. He was pretending to show interest in her to help her gain attention. She'd certainly been successful at that tonight. Of course, Mr. Finch's behavior wasn't the sort of attention she wanted.

She wanted what the duke was doing. He was kind, solicitous, and even flirtatious. This pretend courtship was starting to feel very real.

She only had to remember that it wasn't.

~

The day after the rainstorm, Law spent the late morning with Holden, who was still quite sore from their accident but much happier now that he wasn't lodging with Yates. He felt certain he could go to the stables later that afternoon once he took a rest.

Law had then gone to see what Yates was up to, but the valet had disappeared somewhere.

In the early afternoon, Law had walked around the estate, where he'd encountered Mr. Rowell, the land manager. He was a stoic fellow, but he'd warmed up when Law had queried him about crop rotation and livestock usage—just as Sadie had said he would. Law had learned a few things that he looked forward to implementing.

Now, as he walked back toward the house, he saw Richard coming from the path that led to the stables. Law waited until the young man reached him. "Afternoon, Richard."

"Good afternoon, Your Grace."

"How is my coach?"

"It's coming along well, actually."

Law saw this as an opportunity to get the truth. Of all the Campion brothers, Richard seemed the most transparent. "I was wondering if you have everything you need? Do you, ah, feel confident that you can complete the repair properly? I know this isn't what any of you typically do."

Richard looked down briefly and brushed his hand through his blond hair. "I confess we were somewhat lost without Jarvis." He lifted his gaze to Law's. "He came to the stables this morning and is ensuring everything is done right. It may very well be finished by this evening. If not, tomorrow morning at the latest."

"That's surprising." Perhaps Holden wouldn't need to supervise after all. "I'm pleased to hear it."

"I think Sadie must have spoken with Jarvis. He wasn't happy with our lack of progress when he arrived this morning. He's still there directing things, but then, he'll do anything she asks."

"Jarvis was the coachman before he retired?" Law was fairly certain that was his position, but wanted to make sure.

"Coachman, groom, stable master—everything to do with horses. He still cares for two of them at his own cottage because, like him, they are retired from work. He likes to pretend he's gruff, but he has a soft heart, especially for horses. And Sadie."

"That's why he doesn't say no to her." Law wanted to meet this fellow. "Are they close, then?"

Richard nodded. "He taught her how to ride and drive."

"Did he teach all of you?"

"Yes, but it was different with Sadie. Our father demanded we boys all learn those things, but with Sadie, she was the one who demanded it. So, Jarvis made sure she learned."

Her father seemed bloody ineffectual where she was concerned. "I have no trouble imagining your sister managing her own education. Has she always commanded things?"

Richard laughed, his eyes crinkling at the corners. "*Always.* Especially in my experience, since I don't remember our mother. Sadie has been the only mother figure I've known."

"That must have been a great deal for her to take on since she was only eight when your mother died," Law said softly.

"You know that?" Richard sounded surprised, but quickly nodded. "I suppose you would."

Law ignored the implications of that statement. "What I don't know is why there isn't a house-keeper to alleviate Sadie's burdens. I realize you had one who also died, but that was over a decade ago."

Richard lifted a shoulder. "Sadie wouldn't want to have a housekeeper."

"Are you certain of that?"

"Father and Esmond say so." Richard's eyes rounded briefly. "Speaking of my father, please don't tell him you know the coach is nearly re-paired. He doesn't want you leaving until after the festival."

"Indeed? I would have thought he didn't want me to leave until after I wed your sister," Law didn't disguise his sarcasm.

Richard laughed again, but this time, it carried an uneasiness. "That is what my father hopes, yes. But you mustn't let that influence you," he added earnestly.

Law stifled a smile. "I'll try."

Glancing toward the house, Richard nervously asked, "You promise you won't tell him about the coach? He'll be furious if he finds out I told you."

"I promise. It will be our secret. Anyway, I can't leave because my coachman can't drive until the festival is over."

Richard stared at him. "Certainly a man of your import and station can drive a coach and four. You've been driving the gig to town."

"Of course I can, but now I'll tell *you* a secret. I don't actually want to leave before the festival concludes."

"Because of Sadie." Richard grinned. "You *do* like her. My father will be so happy to hear it."

Law narrowed his eyes at the lad. "I just told you it was a secret. And I didn't mention your sister at all."

Richard's face lost a shade of color, and he straightened as if reprimanded. "My apologies, Your Grace. I promise I won't tell anyone what you said."

"Thank you. I appreciate your discretion. It's an important quality in a gentleman." Law watched the young man puff up. This was something Law's father might have said, but he would have done so in a more demanding way. Here, Law was hoping to ensure the boy's silence on the matter, not encourage him to be strong and unyielding.

"But you do like Sadie, don't you?" Richard's face was so expectant, so hopeful, that Law couldn't deny him.

"I do, in fact." More than he should. Definitely more than he needed to like someone whom he was only pretending to have interest in courting.

"I was sure you did." Richard schooled his features into sobriety. "But I won't say a word." He started toward the house, but instead of accompanying him, Law watched him go.

The lad walked through the kitchen garden, then Sadie came out of the house and spoke with him for a moment before he ducked inside. She went to snip a few herbs, sniffing the clippings before turning to go back into the house.

It was a simple act. She was a simple woman—compared to him and the demands he faced. He envied her.

But this was no place for him. He had responsibilities and a duty that had been generations in the making, including marriage to an "appropriate" woman such as Lady Frederica. His father would be apoplectic to know that Law was here dawdling with Sadie when he ought to be fulfilling his deathbed promise.

This sojourn at Fieldstone was making Law reevaluate his plans. His father wasn't here. At what point could Law claim his life and do entirely what he wanted instead of what was expected? He hadn't realized how much of a hold his father still had on him until this week when he'd found himself torn between meeting his father's demands and pursuing his own desires.

But what did that mean with regard to Sadie? She deserved a simple, kind, hardworking country gentleman who would complement her and give her the life *she* wanted—the life she deserved. And Law would help her achieve that. He could suffer a few more days of unrequited longing.

What would happen to him, then? He'd wed Lady Frederica and forget about Sadie entirely?

He knew in that moment that no matter what happened, he never would.

CHAPTER 7

"I didn't see you all day," Sadie said to the duke as he drove them into Marrywell for the postponed musicale. Though the weather was improved, the performances would take place inside the assembly rooms, just in case.

"I visited with Holden earlier."

"Was Mavis there?" Sadie asked with a chuckle, knowing her maid spent a great deal of time with the coachman.

Lawford sent her a quick smile. "She came in just as I was leaving. Do I need to worry that I shall lose my coachman to Fieldstone?"

Laughing, Sadie shook her head. "I think I'm the one who needs to worry. It's far more likely she'd go with Holden—it's not as if we'd hire him, and I have to think you could find a place for Mavis." She briefly sucked in her lower lip. "Forgive me, that's awfully presumptuous."

"It isn't really. I can see why you'd think that, what with my three houses." He rolled his eyes and grinned, and Sadie was grateful for his sometimes self-deprecating sense of humor.

"Mavis said he's going to attend the Grand Picnic with her tomorrow, though he's apparently disappointed he won't be able to row a boat on the lake because of his arm."

"There's a lake?"

"Yes. Perhaps you wouldn't mind rowing me about?" She saw him grimace faintly—it was so quick that she wondered if she'd imagined it.

"I, ah, I don't particularly like boats. I capsized when I was ten, and it was terrifying. As with the tree, my father insisted I not be afraid of boats, so I'm not. However, I became rather tired of them, so if you're looking for someone to row you about the lake tomorrow, I recommend soliciting one of your admirers."

Sadie laughed. "I'm not sure I have any. I refuse to count that leering Mr. Finch from last night."

"Definitely not." The duke gave her an encouraging smile. "You'll have plenty tonight. I'm sure of it."

"Your confidence is charming, but I'm not convinced this ploy of yours is working. It's already day three of the festival."

"Last night's rainstorm dampened everything, including our plans. Tonight will be more successful. Don't forget that I'm a duke, and I've spent the last decade mastering London Society."

"You'll simply command this evening to be better than the last two? You'll bend all the unmarried men to your will?"

"If I have to."

Sadie laughed. "*There's* the arrogant duke I met. Goodness, was that just two days ago?"

The duke grinned, and her heart did that little flip that stole her breath. "It does feel longer, doesn't it?"

After parking the gig on Garden Street, the duke helped her down. The touch of his hand sent the now expected frisson of excitement up her arm and through the rest of her body so that she fairly thrummed with anticipation. Not for the coming evening but for the next moment when she would get to touch him again by taking his arm. She'd come to look forward to being tucked against him.

He guided her across the street toward the assembly rooms, and as soon as they stepped inside, they garnered a great deal of attention. Conversation slowed or stopped altogether, and people turned to look at them. Sadie wished she had more items in her wardrobe, or at least something to make her ball gowns look as though she weren't wearing the same two over and over. Perhaps she ought to speak with Mavis about making some alterations.

To what end? They didn't have spare funds for wardrobe additions for a once-a-year festival, not when they were saving to buy that adjoining property. And she wasn't going to ask Mavis to spend time adjusting her clothing in the middle of the festival.

Sadie realized the May Queen, Mrs. Martinscroft, was coming straight for her. Petite, with sable hair and bright blue eyes, Mrs. Martinscroft, the daughter of one of the wealthiest landowners in Hampshire, had been an easy choice for maiden fair last year. Then she'd married the most eligible bachelor at the festival—the son of Baron Tippenworth.

Mrs. Martinscroft dipped a curtsey to the duke. "Good evening, Your Grace, Miss Campion." The crown atop her head didn't so much as tilt with her movements. Sadie recalled that the woman, who was probably only a couple of years younger than Sadie, had been incredibly graceful throughout last year's festival. By day three, everyone had assumed she would become the

May Queen. Sometimes, that was the way of things.

This year, there wasn't yet a favorite.

The duke gave the queen a beautifully executed bow. "Good evening, Your Highness."

Sadie imagined him doing that for Queen Charlotte herself, and for a moment, her surroundings faded to gray. How had she found herself in this man's company? Not just in his company, but as his friend? At least, she *thought* they were friends given the manner in which he was helping her and the conversations they'd shared.

"Miss Campion?" The duke's deep voice pulled her back from wherever she'd gone.

Blinking, she summoned a smile. "Good evening, Your Highness." While everyone generally referred to the May Queen as "Your Highness," no one bowed or curtseyed. Until the duke. Sadie wondered if she ought to curtsey.

Thankfully, Mrs. Martinscroft didn't seem to notice or care. "I was hoping you both would sit with Mr. Martinscroft and me this evening."

They would be seated in the center of the front row with the maidens fair around them. Sadie was *not* a maiden fair. Was she going to refuse because she didn't qualify? Wasn't this what she wanted? Even if she wasn't a maiden, the queen's favor in addition to the duke's attention would almost certainly ensure she was at least visible to every unmarried gentleman at the festival. If she couldn't attract a husband in that environment, it was likely she never would.

"That is most kind of you to ask," Sadie said, feeling special in a way she hadn't before. She'd never had close friends in Marrywell. The young women who lived in and around the town attended the quarterly assemblies and spent April to October strolling the botanical gardens—things Sadie didn't do. She'd always been too busy, and frankly, there was usually something she preferred to those things. "Thank you. I just need to take my cloak to the—"

Before she could finish her sentence, Mrs. Martinscroft waved her hand, and a boy of about ten came forward. "Jeremy, please take Miss Campion's cloak."

"Right away, Your Highness." Jeremy took Sadie's cloak, which the duke had removed for her, and hurried away to place it in a cupboard near the entrance hall.

"Who was that?" Lawford asked.

"I neglected to mention the queen has pages. They are boys between eight and ten who serve the queen's needs throughout the week. It's a great honor to be asked. Adam and Richard were pages. Adam only lasted one festival, however. He talked too much."

Mrs. Martinscroft laughed. "That sounds like my younger brother. Come, let's find our seats. Mr. Martinscroft is awaiting us there." She turned and led them into the ballroom, which had a dais for the performers and rows of chairs for the spectators, though not nearly enough for everyone in attendance. Many people would need to stand.

The duke bent his head toward hers as they walked. "This is good, isn't it?"

"Yes." She squeezed his arm, which she'd retaken after he'd removed her cloak. None of this would be happening if not for Law's insistence on helping her. What's more, she hadn't even asked him for his support—he'd offered it enthusiastically. She couldn't help but look at him with a mix of wonder and gratitude. "Thank you for this."

They took their seats, with Mrs. Martinscroft indicating Sadie should sit beside her. *Beside her.* Sadie was in a prime position, *and she wasn't even a maiden fair.* How would she ever thank Law? Providing him lodging and repairing his damaged coach seemed insufficient.

They chatted for several minutes before the mayor spoke from the dais and urged everyone to be seated for the performance. When the room quieted, he introduced the first performers, a quartet from Marrywell who played in the botanical gardens two nights a week during the summer.

After the quartet, there were dancers, then an opera singer, then another group of musicians. At the end, applause filled the ballroom and the mayor returned to the dais.

"Thank you, everyone. Give us a few minutes to move the chairs from the dance floor. Shortly thereafter, the dancing will begin!"

They stood, and Mrs. Martinscroft immediately turned to Sadie and Lawford. "How is your courtship progressing?"

Sadie froze. She hadn't expected a question about that, especially one that was so...explicit. Turning her head slightly, she exchanged a look with the duke.

"We aren't formally courting," he said smoothly. "We are merely getting to know each other."

Mr. Martinscroft, a redheaded gentleman in his late twenties with a few faint freckles on his face gave them a knowing smile, his gaze connecting with the duke's. "I imagine that isn't too difficult since you're sleeping under the same roof."

Was he implying something...scandalous? No, he couldn't be.

The page, Jeremy, interrupted them. "Pardon

me, Your Highness. You'll need to move while they remove the chairs."

"Of course," Mrs. Martinscroft murmured. She took Sadie's arm and guided her away from the seating area, which was also the dance floor. "I think you and the duke must start the dancing tonight."

Sadie nearly tripped. "But I'm not a maiden fair. They always start the dancing."

"There's been an occasional departure from tradition. I remember a few years ago when Mr. and Mrs. Armstrong started the dancing."

That was because it had been their fortieth wedding anniversary, but Sadie wasn't going to point that out. Who was she to question the May Queen?

"I'd say having a duke in attendance necessitates a slight bending of the rules. It seems appropriate to have him start the dancing at least one night, and while he could ask one of the seven maidens, I daresay he'd rather ask you." She turned her head to look at Lawford, who was following behind them with Mr. Martinscroft. "Isn't that right, Your Grace?"

"I am honored to do whatever you ask, Your Highness."

Sadie chewed the inside of her lip to keep from frowning. Did that mean he didn't want to dance with her? She immediately chastised herself for that thought. He'd offered to help her snare a husband and was doing a splendid job of elevating her status. Of course he would dance with her. He'd also said many other things that led her to think he would want to dance with *her*. She still couldn't quite believe it, however.

At the side of the room, the thrones from the crowning ceremony had been arranged in a row.

Several of the maidens fair had already gathered there.

Sadie took her arm from Mrs. Martinscroft as they came to a stop and turned to the duke, mostly so she could avoid looking at the maidens. She'd been about to ask if he wanted to dance, but that was his role, not hers.

"Miss Campion, I would be honored if you would dance with me." He offered her his hand.

"It would be my honor as well." She curtseyed and put her hand in his, eager for the electrical current she knew and expected.

He tucked her hand over his arm and strolled back toward the dance floor, which had somehow already been cleared of chairs. "You didn't have to curtsey," he said.

"Why not? You didn't have to bow to the queen either."

"Is that not done?"

"Not typically. I fear now you will have started a new tradition, however. Everyone will take the duke's lead, no doubt."

"Do you see the burden I carry?" he asked drily, prompting her to laugh. "Think what might have happened if I'd sneezed at the wrong moment."

"You poor thing." She patted his arm with her free hand as they moved onto the dance floor.

The musicians who'd performed last were providing the music, and they appeared ready to begin. The maidens fair and their partners joined them, and they formed two lines with Sadie and Law at the top.

When the music started, Sadie and Law met and danced between the others, moving toward the end. It was nearly impossible to talk when dancing in this manner, but Sadie was dying to ask about

Mr. Martinscroft's comment. "Did you hear what Martinscroft said?"

"About us sleeping under the same roof?" At her nod, Law's gaze darkened just before it darted across the room to where the thrones—and Martinscroft—were located. "He's lucky we were in a public space, or I would have put him in his place."

Law's expression and tone reminded her of last night in the folly when he'd scared away Mr. Finch. It also recalled how she'd thought him haughty upon meeting him.

She looked up at him as they neared the end of the line. "You can be rather intimidating."

"Is that a compliment?" His eyes glittered beneath the sparkling candlelight overhead.

Sadie wasn't able to determine if he was asking her in earnest or being coy. She also wasn't sure how to answer that. Fortunately, she didn't have to, because they had to separate back into the line.

As the others took their turns, she and the duke would intermittently lock gazes. Each time, she felt a pull to move toward him. Then she would look away and see everyone staring at them. At one point, she caught sight of her father, who was watching her with an odd smile.

Suddenly, she realized that *this* was what she wanted, to feel beautiful and important. Desirable.

What nonsense! She didn't need those things. What she wanted was a husband and a home with a family of her own. Once again, her gaze met Law's. How she wished he wasn't a duke. Why couldn't he be someone she actually could share forever with?

The dance ended, and the duke bowed while she curtseyed. He guided her from the dance floor, and she was immediately met by a handful of gentlemen seeking her next dances, a few of them from last night and a couple of them new.

She looked to Law, who gave her a small smile before leaning toward her. "I'll see you later. Enjoy tonight."

His cheek had been so close to hers that she could feel his heat. If she'd moved a few inches, she could have pressed her lips to his.

But no. Not here. And not him.

She arranged to dance with all five gentlemen and immediately returned to the dance floor with the first one. This was what she *needed*—a chance to be seen so that she could wed.

Before it was too late.

~

Last night, Law and Sadie had been among some of the last people to leave the assembly rooms. On the ride home, she'd dozed off, her head falling against Law's shoulder. Her warm presence against him had made him feel surprisingly content. He honestly couldn't ever recall such a sensation.

When they'd arrived at Fieldstone, he'd gently awakened her, and she'd been adorably startled, especially when she realized she'd been sleeping *on* him. She'd apologized profusely and had quickly made her way upstairs. He hoped she didn't feel badly about it and planned to mention it to her today.

He'd slept later than usual and taken breakfast in his room. After bathing and refusing further skin-care experimentation from Yates, Law was now dressed and ready for this afternoon's Grand Picnic.

He left his room, eager to get downstairs to meet Sadie. Instead, he ran straight into her father, who—for once—wore a disgruntled expression.

"I require a few minutes of your time, Your Grace," he said sternly.

The man's pique didn't alarm Law in the slightest. After enduring his father's changeable moods, which had become increasingly more frequent since his mother had died, it took a great deal to affect him.

"Always happy to entertain my host," Law said with a bland smile.

"This isn't entertaining for me. I'm afraid I must ask your intentions toward my daughter."

Law needed to be careful. He had to tread between committing to a courtship to maintain their ruse and being noncommittal lest he find himself leg-shackled to a woman he was not supposed to marry. "We're getting to know each other as I squire her to these matchmaking events."

Campion frowned, forming deep jowls on the sides of his face. "Are you going to marry Sadie or not? Because there are a great many gentlemen seeking her attention. Two of them called this morning and left flowers."

Had they? Law wanted to ask what Sadie had thought of that, but it wasn't his business. They were achieving the desired results, and that was all that mattered, even if jealousy was nipping at his heels. "How wonderful for her."

"It would be more wonderful if it were *you* giving her flowers," Campion grumbled.

"I should think you would be happy that she is being noticed and appreciated."

"Yes, yes, I am glad for that, but she has an opportunity to be a duchess. What father wouldn't want that for his daughter?"

Two things occurred to Law. One, anyone who assumed that a duke who happened to suffer a mishap in front of their house and required assistance would offer an *opportunity* to wed their daughter did not have two feet planted in reality. Two, was it possible Campion was finally feeling a modicum of guilt at ignoring his daughter's marriage prospects and allowing her to work tirelessly for him and his household while she was pushed more and more firmly upon a shelf?

It was difficult for Law to separate his reaction. He had trouble ignoring his father's teachings, which said a duke would never consider marrying someone so far beneath his rank. But he also couldn't deny that he understood Campion's desire to see his daughter wed to someone so far above her position. The potential for her, especially someone as clever and confident as Miss Campion, was great. There was also the simple fact that regardless of rank or acceptability, Law liked and admired her. Perhaps most compelling of all—he wanted her in a most visceral way.

"I can understand that," Law finally replied. "However, neither of us has decided if we will suit."

"The festival is more than half over at the end of today's picnic. Many gentlemen will begin to make their moves. You don't want to be left empty-handed."

Law swallowed a laugh. As if a duke couldn't marry at will. God, that sounded like his father. Anyway, the point was that Law wouldn't lose the possibility of a wife, he'd specifically lose *Sadie*. And yes, that stirred a fervent jealousy, though he tried to ignore it.

But in the end, this wasn't about him. It was about helping Sadie. Law crossed his arms over his chest and pinned Campion with an intense stare. "Would there be anything wrong with her marrying someone other than me? What if she falls hopelessly in love with a gentleman she danced with last night? Surely, you'd be happy for her even if he didn't have a lofty title. Or is that all that matters to you?"

Campion sputtered. "Of course not."

Law had him on the defensive now. Good. Perhaps the man would reconsider his motives. Perhaps he'd reconsider his entire relationship with his wonderful, underappreciated daughter. "What if my coach hadn't lost a wheel outside your house? Would you still be encouraging Sadie to attend all the festival events? Would you be hopeful she might find love so that she will have a secure future?"

Grinning, Campion clapped his hands together. "You called her Sadie."

Had he? Law stared at him. "Did you hear anything else I said?"

"Ah, yes, of course. I'm thrilled you are spending time with my daughter, and I'm confident you'll decide she'll make an excellent duchess." He patted Law on the arm, then turned to go downstairs.

Watching him depart, Law wondered how the man had raised such a competent and spectacular daughter. He went downstairs to wait for Sadie in the parlor. Her father was there along with Adam and Richard.

"Ah, here she is," Campion said, his gaze moving past Law.

Law pivoted to see Sadie framed in the doorway. Garbed in the presumably mended rose-colored gown that she'd torn on the first day, she took his breath away. The bodice was trimmed with a pretty ivory ribbon, and flowers were embroidered in the same color across the front. She wore a cunning straw hat adorned with silk roses.

"How lovely you look today, Miss Campion."

Law was careful not to call her Sadie again. "You shall command everyone's attention at the Grand Picnic."

"It looks as though she's already commanded yours," Campion said with a hearty laugh.

Law clenched his jaw before smiling at Sadie and offering his arm. "Shall we be on our way?"

"Yes, thank you."

He escorted her from the house without a backward glance for her father.

CHAPTER 8

The day of the Grand Picnic was the nicest of the festival so far, which was lucky since the event was, of course, held outside at the botanical gardens. Blankets were arranged near the lake, which was almost in the middle of the gardens. A road circuited the property, with a few other tracks crossing it here and there, one of which led to the lake. After parking the gig, Law gave a coin to the boy who came forward to say he would watch the horse.

Sadie took his arm. "I've seen you do that a few times now—when we are either coming or going."

Law shrugged. "The lads are working hard. Seems like they deserve some small reward."

"You're very kind. And generous. I have to think your parents would be very proud of you."

"I always hoped they would be." The response was a little odd, as if he wasn't sure that was true. He paused at the top of the slope that led down to the lake. "Look at all the blankets."

Was he trying to change the subject? He was probably just genuinely surprised. "This is the most attended event of the entire festival," she explained. "If anyone at Marrywell is at home today, it's because they are ill."

"I see. Besides the rowboats on the lake, I understand there is a badminton tournament."

Sadie nodded as they walked down the gently rolling hill. "There are other games too. There's an entire area just for children. When I was young, we looked forward to this day all year."

Smiling, Lawford glanced down at her. "I must admit, this is an incredibly charming festival. And town."

"Sadie! Come join us!" Esmond's wife, Annabelle, was beckoning for them to come to the blanket where she sat with Esmond and Philip and Philip's wife, Janet.

"We may as well," Sadie said to Law. "Finding a blanket can be difficult, and we'll have to share with someone."

"That's a shame."

She snapped her head toward him. "Why is that?"

"I mean no offense to your family. I only meant it would be nice to have our own blanket."

Did he really think so? Why?

"I confess I'm not used to sharing," he added. "But mostly, I just enjoy your company."

Smiling, Sadie tried not to bounce too much as they walked to the blanket, where they exchanged pleasantries with Sadie's brothers and their wives.

Before Sadie and Law could sit down, Mr. Jacob Atkins, a gentleman she'd danced with last night, approached. Not much older than Sadie, he seemed nervous. He was tall and slim with long arms and a thick mop of dark hair beneath his hat. His gaze darted toward the duke before he settled on Sadie. "I wonder if you might like to go out in a rowboat with me, Miss Campion?"

Sadie looked to the duke, knowing he didn't like boats. He gave a slight nod, jutting his chin toward the lake, seeming to silently communicate that she should go.

Belatedly, she wondered why she'd even looked toward him. He wasn't her keeper, and the goal was for her to find a husband that wasn't him. Perhaps she'd done so because he'd told her he wanted a blanket to themselves. That he'd wanted that still intrigued her.

Turning her attention back to the young man, she smiled. "Thank you, that would be lovely."

Over the course of the next hour or more, Sadie took three boat rides with three different gentlemen. A fourth asked for yet another ride, but she politely declined, instead saying he could escort her back to her blanket for a needed respite. They'd detoured to the refreshment tables, where he'd fetched her a glass of lemonade. When they reached the blanket, he said he hoped to see her later.

Sadie sat down and finished the lemonade in one long drink. "Goodness, I'm in need of a rest."

"How can being rowed around in a boat exhaust you?" Annabelle asked. "You are the most inexhaustible person I know."

Sadie ignored Annabelle's comment and asked where the duke and her brothers were.

"They are in the brewer's field sampling beer." Annabelle waved her hand in a vague direction. "It's over near the children's area. Thank goodness my parents have taken the boys to play. Now, *they* are exhausting."

Sadie went to take another sip of lemonade, then realized her glass was empty. *Blast.* She didn't really want to get up to fetch more.

Annabelle fixed her with an expectant stare.

"Why are you rowing around the lake with anyone other than the duke? If I were you, I'd be pasted to his side."

To avoid answering the question, Sadie reached for a basket of biscuits on the blanket. "Are these Mrs. Rowell's?"

"Yes, and a few others. The boys picked far too many from the biscuit table. Eat all you like." Annabelle readjusted herself on the blanket, fanning her skirt out prettily.

Janet leaned toward Sadie. "I don't understand why you are bothering with other gentlemen when the duke is courting you."

"He's not courting me. There has been no official declaration. He's being kind, escorting me to the festival. I think he feels he should in exchange for our hospitality."

Annabelle arched a blonde brow. "In what ways are you being *hospitable*?"

Sadie resisted the urge to groan. "Please don't make assumptions. He's our guest—by necessity. If there were any room at an inn in town, he would take it."

"I could give you some advice," Annabelle offered. "To ensure a proposal is forthcoming." Her gaze dipped to Sadie's chest. "We could just tighten up your corset and pull down that bodice a wee bit."

Sadie leapt up. Perhaps she could find that fourth gentleman and take another boat ride. Or just jump into the lake. Anything that wasn't sitting here listening to her sisters-in-law. "I think I need more lemonade." She held up her empty glass, then turned and went in the direction of the refreshments.

After pouring more lemonade and downing it in just a few gulps, she left the empty glass on a tray. Pivoting, she was shocked to see the May Queen standing there.

"Good afternoon, Miss Campion. Are you enjoying the Grand Picnic?"

"Yes, thank you, Your Highness. And you?"

"I'm so pleased the weather has cooperated." She grinned. "It's as if the heavens knew I wanted to make this a Grand Picnic to remember."

Sadie couldn't recall anything the queen did as part of the Grand Picnic besides walk around and be seen and sit on the most prominent blanket at the top of the hill. "Oh?"

Mrs. Martinscroft motioned for Sadie to step away from the table with her. This was a fairly good vantage point of the array of picnic blankets, with the sparkling lake off to the right. "I'm going to make an announcement, and it involves you." Her eyes gleamed with anticipation.

Sadie didn't get a chance to ask what this was about before Mrs. Martinscroft addressed the picnic in a surprisingly loud voice. "Good afternoon, my dear Marrywellers and guests! What a splendid day for our Grand Picnic!" This was greeted by loud cheers, and it was a moment before the queen could continue. "I'm thrilled to announce the first ever special *eighth* maiden fair. Please join me in congratulating the fair Miss Sadie Campion!" She turned to face Sadie and clapped.

There was a beat of silence. Sadie held her breath. Was this really happening?

Then there were more cheers, and Sadie realized it was. "I…I don't know what to say," she managed, but only loud enough for Mrs. Martinscroft to hear.

"Thank you is just fine," the queen responded softly with a bright laugh.

"Thank you."

"I'm sorry I don't have a flower crown for you, but you'll have one before the day is out. The woman who makes them was busy with her grand-children in the children's area. I'm not at all certain they can find an eighth throne, however. At least not one that matches."

"That's…fine. Thank you. This is…unexpected."

Mrs. Martinscroft looked about. "Where is your duke? I was certain he'd come forward to join you. Let me summon him."

"That won't be necessary. I know where he is." Had he heard the announcement? Probably not. Sadie couldn't even see the brewers' area from here, and Mrs. Martinscroft hadn't spoken *that* loudly. Sadie felt unaccountably disappointed that he wasn't here. "And he isn't *my* duke," she said.

Why did everyone think their betrothal was all but finalized? She was a squire's daughter, and he was a *duke*, for heaven's sake.

"Perhaps not yet. Just think, if you become be-trothed, you may very well be next year's queen. Oh my, it looks as though some people want to congratulate you."

Sadie watched as perhaps two dozen people moved toward them. Panic surged in her chest. Wasn't this what she'd always wanted? Where was Law? His presence made her feel secure. Protected.

Besides, she wanted to share this with him. Without his help, none of this would be happening.

Everything around her seemed to freeze, as if the world came to a halt. Without the duke, she was just Miss Sadie Campion, who would likely never have had a chance to be a maiden fair. Without him and his attention, she was…nothing.

"Pardon me," she murmured before dashing away from the approaching hordes. She walked quickly, but then ran, veering from the path into a stand of trees.

The brush was fairly thick, so she didn't get far. Still, it was dim and quiet, and she had a moment to think.

Breathing deeply to catch her breath, she stared at the tree in front of her. Did she really think she was nothing? Of course not, but she had to wonder how desirable she was without Lawford at her side.

She allowed herself to remember her first festival as a young lady eligible for matchmaking. That had been four years ago. She'd met Walter Osborne, a dashing gentleman from Bath. With dark curls and fathomless blue eyes that had seemed to see straight into Sadie's soul, he'd fooled her into thinking he'd cared for her. She'd thought they were courting, for they'd danced together several times and then they'd kissed and touched in the labyrinth. When he'd wanted to take more liberties than she was comfortable allowing, he'd seemed to understand her preference to wait until they were wed. Except, he'd ignored her for the remaining two days of the festival and certainly hadn't offered the proposal she'd expected.

Confused and distraught, she'd confronted him on the last day, and he'd laughed in her face. Then she'd asked a few of the other girls if she'd been wrong to expect a proposal. They'd also laughed and asked how she couldn't see that Walter hadn't been serious, that he'd come to the festival to have fun. After all, Sadie wasn't the only girl he'd kissed...

Squeezing her eyes shut, Sadie clenched her fists and counted to ten. She breathed in and out until the old fury died away.

This was not four years ago. And the duke was absolutely *not* Walter Osborne.

A few minutes ago, she'd experienced the thrill of her life. All of Marrywell and plenty of guests from elsewhere had cheered her appointment as the first-ever eighth maiden fair. *Her.* Sadie Campion. A maiden fair! But would it have happened without the duke? She didn't think so, and now she felt worse than if she'd never been chosen.

Especially now that she realized her failure to wed this year would be witnessed by everyone since she was a maiden fair. Except Law had promised her that she *would* marry. He couldn't guarantee that, not unless he wanted to marry her himself. And *that* had certainly never come up, nor did she expect it to.

She wasn't sure how long she stood in the small forest, but it was actually rather cool, and she began to shiver. With some reluctance, she made her way back toward the path.

"Sadie?"

Law's voice reached her before she saw him, as she was still a few feet from the path. She emerged from the trees as he walked in front of her, his features creasing with relief. "There you are," he said. "Mrs. Martinscroft said you'd come this way, but I couldn't find you. Why did you run off? I wanted to congratulate you on your appointment to maiden fair. Actually, a great many wanted to do so. I said I'd find you and bring you back."

"I wish you hadn't done that." She sounded grumpy, and she didn't care.

His brow furrowed. "What's wrong? I thought you'd be ecstatic."

"I was. For a moment. Then I realized the truth —that without you, I have no worth at all. No one would be paying me attention, and I certainly wouldn't be a maiden fair."

"That's not true at all."

"Prove it."

His gaze held her captive, so that she felt she couldn't move. Nor did she want to.

He moved closer, until there was barely any space between them at all. "You have more worth than most people I've met. You're intelligent, caring, selfless, as well as incomparably beautiful." He lifted his hand to her face and gently caressed her cheek.

Sadie's knees turned to water. She had to brace herself by putting her hands on his chest. "Are you going to kiss me?"

He glanced at her mouth. "If you'll allow it."

"May I demand it?"

Sliding his hand to her nape, he bent his head and pressed his lips to hers. She curled her hands around his lapels, holding on to him as if she might be carried away by the sudden swell of desire that crashed over her.

His other hand came around her waist and pulled her against him. She didn't want her hands between them, so she pushed them up and clasped his shoulders. She had to stand on her toes because he was so tall.

He cupped her head as he slanted his mouth over hers. His tongue licked along her lower lip, and she opened her mouth, eager to taste him.

She dug her fingers into his coat as he swept his tongue along hers. The kiss aroused countless sensations, all centered around an insistent throb between her legs.

They moved together, exploring with their hands and mouths, until Sadie felt restless and desperate. She wanted more.

He kissed along her jaw and neck, making her gasp with longing. "You can't tell me no one noticed you before I arrived." He spoke between kisses.

Sadie clutched at his head as his lips trailed along the edge of her bodice. "Not the way they have this week," she managed breathlessly. Because she'd been hiding at Fieldstone.

He lifted his head, his dark eyes searing her with a sensual heat. "That, to me, is a crime."

She wanted to kiss him again, to lose herself in the delicious haze that had begun to settle over her. But she saw movement from the corner of her eye and realized they'd been found. "People are coming."

He quickly stepped back. "I doubt they saw anything. My back was to them. Just take my arm, and we'll walk as if nothing happened."

Except something had happened, something life changing. This might not have been Sadie's first kiss, but she would have been happy if it had been her last. Only she didn't want that either. She wanted more kisses—from him.

Though she felt a bit shaky, Sadie took his arm. They walked along the path toward the people coming their way. Among them were her younger brothers, but not her father. At least not that she could see.

Glancing over at Law, she wondered if he'd been as affected as her. Would he want to kiss her again? Unfortunately, now was not the time she could find out.

~

Following the Grand Picnic, Law had returned to Fieldstone with the intent of bathing and then joining Sadie at the gardens that evening. She'd remained in town with the other maidens fair to prepare for the evening. It was tradition for them to gather at the New Inn, the largest and oldest lodging in Marrywell, which also served as the unofficial headquarters of the May Court, to ready themselves between events. However, after indulging in a tea tray following his bath, Law began to feel unwell and had collapsed into bed. He hadn't stirred until that morning. If he didn't know better, he would have thought he'd taken laudanum.

This morning, he was completely recovered and keen to find Sadie so that he could explain his absence. He also wanted to find out how her evening went. Most of all, he was eager to speak with her about the kiss they'd shared yesterday afternoon. He'd awakened thinking of that delightful encounter, his body thick with desire.

A disturbing sense of betrayal lingered at the back of his mind—because of his impending meeting with the Earl of Gillingham and the man's daughter. With each day that Law spent at Fieldstone, he became less and less interested in fulfilling his father's dying demand. And now that he'd kissed Sadie, things had most definitely shifted. He couldn't very well carry on with her—or long for her—when he had this potential betrothal hanging over his head.

He knew in that moment that he didn't even want to meet Lady Frederica. He wanted to be right here at Fieldstone, continuing to get to know Sadie. If he could find a messenger, he would send word to Gillingham notifying him that he wouldn't be able to meet his daughter after all.

The conclusion of the festival brought its own worries. If things went according to plan, Sadie would be betrothed—and not to him. This result was growing more and more distasteful. If Law was having trouble watching her dancing with other gentlemen, how could he see her wed one of them?

It seemed he had some decisions to make regarding courtship and perhaps even marriage. The thought of that was both dizzyingly exciting and somewhat terrifying. He'd only just met Sadie, and yet he was genuinely considering if she'd want to be his duchess. Would she want that? Was he certain he wanted that?

He nearly walked past a narrow open cupboard on his way to the stairs, but caught sight of Sadie inside organizing linens. He stepped into the doorway. "Good morning."

She startled, her shoulders jerking as she turned to face him with slightly widened eyes. "Law, I didn't hear you. Good morning." She smiled warmly as she tucked some linens onto a shelf. Facing him, she asked, "How are you feeling? Papa said you didn't come last night because you were ill. I hope it wasn't anything terrible. You seemed fine at the picnic."

He realized he was blocking the light from the corridor and moved into the cupboard to the left side. The closet became quite snug as they both occupied the small space. "The malaise came on rather quickly. I had tea with some of Mrs. Rowell's scrumptious cakes, then promptly felt most unwell. I apologize for missing last night. I feel dreadful that I wasn't there to support you."

She'd pivoted as he'd come into the cupboard. Now they faced each other with not even a foot between them. "It's quite all right. I completely understand." Her gaze quickly flicked toward his mouth. So quickly that he wondered if he'd imagined it.

He managed to keep himself from looking at

her mouth, which was difficult since yesterday's kiss was at the forefront of his mind. "Still, I made a promise to help you, and I wasn't able to." He felt more than dreadful—he was thoroughly annoyed with himself. "How was your evening?" He hesitated, but forced himself to ask about her progress. "What I really mean is, how goes the happiness hunting?"

"Very well, thank you. But I did miss you." There! She did it again. Her gaze shot to his mouth and lingered for the barest moment. There was no mistaking it that time.

He had to work to keep his mind from entertaining thoughts of taking her in his arms, of kissing her. Taking a breath that wasn't anywhere deep enough, he asked, "Has any particular gentleman captivated your interest?"

It took her a moment to answer, and in that span of time, the air in the cupboard thickened and warmed. "I think so, perhaps." Again, she looked at his mouth, and Law couldn't stand it any longer.

He inched toward her. "I keep thinking about yesterday in the forest. We should not have done that."

"Why?" she asked, her gaze holding his. "I have no regrets, and I would feel better if you didn't either." Her hand grazed his.

He threaded his fingers with hers, and they moved closer to one another. "Then I won't."

"I keep thinking about it too," she said softly. "I have to go to the gardens this afternoon."

Was she asking him a question? "I am taking a ride with Rowell," he said, now wishing he hadn't arranged that.

A shadow dimmed her gaze, but it was quickly gone. Was she disappointed? Perhaps he should change his plans. "Will you come to the festival tonight?" she asked.

"Do you want me to?" If she'd met a gentleman, he ought to stay out of her way. Except...she was holding his hand and looking at him as if she wanted to repeat yesterday's kisses.

"I missed your company last night." She stroked his hand with her thumb.

Law itched to put his hand around her, to pull her against him, to press his lips to her cheek, her throat, her delectable mouth. "Then I will be there. Mayhap you can finally show me the labyrinth."

A second shadow darkened her features, but this one didn't dissipate as quickly.

Tugging on her hand, he moved closer and tipped his head down. "Did I say something wrong?"

She shook her head. Then she stood on her toes, bringing her mouth toward his.

"Sadie," he whispered.

"Pardon me."

Law and Sadie jerked apart and faced the doorway. Mavis stood just outside—there was no room for her to come in—with faintly pink cheeks. Her gaze was trained somewhere past them in the depths of the cupboard.

Moving out of the cupboard, Law sidestepped Mavis, who edged out of his way. "I'll see you later," he said to Sadie before hastening back to his chamber.

Yates was there tidying up after Law's toilet. "Back so soon?"

"Er, yes, I forgot something."

Arching a gray brow, Yates contemplated Law's appearance. "What's that?"

"My hat," he said quickly. "I'm going for a walk." He needed air, as well as to be alone with his thoughts to contemplate what the devil was going on between him and Sadie.

Yates handed him his hat and narrowed his eyes. "Are you all right, Your Grace? You seem out of sorts."

"I'm fine." Law ground out the words.

"This place must be adversely affecting you." Yates gave him a knowing nod. "I am most eager to depart. I'm sure you must feel the same. I've no doubt your father would have found a way to be on his way immediately. He would have wanted you to do the same—to fulfill your duty."

Law turned on his heel and left without answering.

No, he was not eager to leave. He liked Fieldstone and Marrywell and their surprisingly charming festival, and most of all, he liked Sadie. The thought of leaving, of going back to his—what now seemed—empty life filled him with dread.

More and more, it seemed Sadie might be the woman he hadn't yet found—the woman he could fall in love with. If he hadn't already.

Law wasn't yet sure, but he was absolutely going to find out.

CHAPTER 9

It was still light when Sadie and the other maidens fair entered the gardens in a procession that evening. People lined the path as the maidens made their way to the dais where their thrones were arranged. Well, seven wrought iron chairs decorated with flowers in addition to the brass thrones belonging to the king and queen. Sadie's small wooden chair looked rather...sad. At least it had flowers tonight.

The mayor introduced them from the stage, then announced that the dancing would commence at eight. Until then, people would stroll and converse. They'd also drink ale and wine and perhaps eat if they were so inclined. Sadie wouldn't eat as she was too afraid that she'd ruin her new gown.

Mavis had surprised her with a ball gown purchased by Sadie's father from the only modiste in town. The dark yellow-gold gown was trimmed with crimson ribbon, and Mavis had entwined matching ribbon into Sadie's hair. Her flower crown was made of yellow and red flowers. Sadie truly felt like a maiden fair. She'd been overcome by her father's shocking extravagance and grateful for Mavis's hard work to coordinate everything.

As Sadie left the dais following the introductions, she encountered a gentleman she'd met last night. Mr. Marmaduke Stackhouse was of average height, with thick brown hair, bright sherry-colored eyes, and an easy smile.

He bowed to her and asked if she would care to promenade.

Sadie hadn't yet seen Law arrive. If she had, would she have declined Mr. Stackhouse's invitation?

She couldn't afford to do that. Mr. Stackhouse was kind, charming, and he owned a large, profitable farm about thirty miles from Marrywell.

Smiling, Sadie put her hand on his arm. "I'd be delighted." Touching him gave her none of the giddy anticipation that just being near Law offered, but she needed to not compare them.

"I enjoyed our row around the lake earlier today," Mr. Stackhouse said, referring to that afternoon when he'd taken her out in a boat.

"We were fortunate as the boats are typically only available the day of the Grand Picnic. However, I understand they wanted to have them out today to make up for the rain that ruined the other night's activities."

"Perhaps I'm glad I arrived late to the festival," he said as they walked along the path. Pages were lighting torches and lanterns to prepare for the coming darkness. "I heard it rained quite hard."

"It did indeed." Sadie recalled what he'd told her about why he was late—one of his cows had delivered a calf, and it had been difficult. He hadn't wanted to leave until he was certain all was well. "Have you thought of a name for your new calf?"

she asked. He'd mentioned that he was still considering what that ought to be.

"It should probably be Lucky or Fortune," he said with a laugh. "But I was also thinking May or Marrywell in honor of your lovely town and festival."

"If you do decide on one of those, you'll need to tell the mayor, Mr. Armstrong. He'll be thrilled."

"I'll keep that in mind." He slid her a brilliant smile. "Now, tell me—have I ruined my chances to find a bride by missing half the festival?"

"Not at all. But only you can decide, of course. Honestly, a week is a rather rushed courtship," she said with a light laugh.

"Are you saying a three-and-a-half-day—and that's being generous—courtship isn't wise? I can't say I disagree."

"I suppose the length of time doesn't matter so much as the connection. If it's right and true, and both parties recognize that, what difference does it make if it's a day or a year?"

He paused and regarded her with a spark of admiration in his gaze. "I wholly concur, Miss Campion. When the dancing begins, would you allow me to be your first partner?"

Sadie hesitated. He was the most pleasant and... real man she'd met so far. But he wasn't Law. After kissing Law yesterday and this morning's near kiss, she was struggling to think of any man but him.

However, she could not afford to do that. He'd promised to help her find a husband, and perhaps Mr. Stackhouse was that man.

Instead of making her happy, the thought filled her with disappointment.

Oh dear, he was waiting for her answer. "I would be delighted to start the dancing with you."

They continued their promenade until the mayor announced it was time for the dancing to commence. As Mr. Stackhouse led her to the dance floor, she saw Law standing off to the side. His gaze followed her, and she was as aware of his presence as she'd been that morning in the cupboard.

Following the dance, she thanked Mr. Stackhouse who said he hoped to see her later. Sadie returned the sentiment but mostly because she was in a hurry to get to Law and would have said anything.

As Sadie approached Law, his gaze moved over her slowly, lingeringly, making her feel as though he noted every single part of her. "Good evening, Miss Campion. Or should I call you Lady Maiden Fair?"

"You may call me whatever you prefer. Do you like my new gown?" She turned from side to side, the skirt moving with her.

"I was going to ask if it was new, but then I realized that would indicate I am far too aware of your garments."

She cocked her head. "Is that bad?"

He gave her a sly look. "You tell me."

"No." It made her feel special. She realized they were flirting and that she'd never really done it before. Not like this, not when she knew what it would be like to kiss him and when she hoped it would happen again.

"Your Grace! Miss Campion!" Mr. Armstrong strode toward them, his wife on his arm. "I hope you're enjoying this fine evening. We've had remarkable luck with the weather the past two days. Let's hope it holds out for the remainder of the festival." Mr. Armstrong turned to Lawford, his dark eyes narrowing slightly with eager intent. "Speaking of that. Your Grace, I wondered if you would do us the honor of serving as a judge for tomorrow's pudding competition."

A quick smile lifted Lawford's lips. "I'd be delighted. In fact, I was hoping you'd ask. I do enjoy a good pudding."

"Splendid!" The mayor looked over at his wife. "Did you hear that, dear?"

"I did." Mrs. Armstrong, a reedy woman in her fifties with a warm hazel gaze and pale blonde hair, gave Lawford a grateful smile. "We deeply appreciate it. It's been our distinct pleasure to have you at the festival this week. I understand you hadn't planned to come, that your coach suffered an accident, but perhaps it's been a fruitful week?" She glanced toward Sadie with a hopeful expression.

Sadie wondered how he would respond. It seemed an obvious attempt to determine if the duke had found a match.

"I've enjoyed myself," he said rather blandly, and though Sadie knew he had to say something like that, she still suffered a pang of disappointment.

Was she really beginning to think she could wed a duke? She needed to get her head out of the clouds.

"Be sure to report to the assembly rooms by one tomorrow afternoon," Mrs. Armstrong said. "And thank you again!"

Sadie watched them walk away and murmured, "You evaded that question well enough."

"What should I have said?"

"Precisely what you did." She was telling herself that as much as him.

He scowled after the Armstrongs. "I can't stand overly inquisitive people. In instances like that, they're only fishing for information they can share."

"Do you regret agreeing to judge the pudding competition?" she asked.

"Not at all. I meant what I said. I'm glad to be a part of this festival and its traditions. This is a major departure from what I'm used to," he said wryly. "The scale of it all is staggering. Your town should be commended."

Though Sadie had next to nothing to do with the festival or its success, she was thrilled to hear him complimenting her home. "It's difficult not to fall in love with Marrywell. It's lovely even when it's not the May Day week."

"I would say I have fallen in love," he said, lifting a brow. "Though, I've yet to see everything to make my final assessment. I'm still anticipating seeing the labyrinth with you."

Blast. Sadie had hoped he would forget about that.

He fixed his gaze on her, his eyes narrowing slightly. "There. You did it again."

"Did what?"

"Your brow gathered, and a shadow passed over your features as if a dark cloud had situated itself right over your head. Why don't you like the labyrinth?"

"It isn't that I don't like it."

"Do you mean that in the way that I don't like boats? Did something happen there?" He looked suddenly alarmed.

Exhaling, Sadie decided she might as well tell him the truth. "Four years ago at my first festival as an eligible bride, I met a suave gentleman. His name was Walter Osborne, and he'd come from Bath to search for a wife. He was charming and attentive, and we danced the second and third nights. Then, on the fourth night, we went into the labyrinth together." She took Lawford's arm and started walking, giving him no choice but to go along. She needed to be doing something other than looking at him to reveal the next part.

"Why do I think I'm going to be angry at where this story goes?"

"I hope you aren't, though I expect your opinion of me may plummet." She wished she hadn't started to tell him. What had she been thinking?

He paused, turning toward her and looking into her eyes. "Nothing you say would cause that to happen. *Nothing.* I won't judge you. If you've changed your mind about telling me, that's fine, but I'd like to know why the labyrinth bothers you."

Sadie could have melted in his gaze. He was so kind, so understanding, so supportive. Of course she could tell him. She started walking once more because she still didn't want to be facing him when she said it out loud. "I knew that girls—young ladies—who went into the labyrinth often kissed young men. Perhaps even older men." She shrugged. "At your first festival, you're giddy and reckless. At least I was. It led to utterly foolish behavior."

"You allowed him to kiss you?"

She nodded. "And…touch me. He wanted to lift my skirts, but I wouldn't let him go that far. I said he'd have to wait until we were wed. He said he understood, but then the next day, he ignored me completely."

Lawford said something under his breath, and Sadie would have sworn it was a curse. "Where is this bounder so I may introduce him to my fist?"

Pausing again, she looked over at him. "Why do

you feel a need to resort to violence with every man who oversteps with me?"

"I'm afraid that's how I was raised. 'Always protect women and never allow bounders to get away with bad behavior. More importantly, never miss an opportunity to show your superiority.'" He grimaced. "I don't give a damn about that last one, but it's what was hammered into my head."

"You're a duke. I'd say your superiority is on constant display."

He brushed his palm over his cheek with another grimace. "You're right, and I know that. For some reason, I feel particularly protective of you. My wanting to toss that Finch fellow on his arse the other night and hoping I might someday have an opportunity to ruin Osborne's day is entirely because I want to avenge you."

How could she not feel flattered? And giddy, but hopefully not in a way that would entice her to act foolishly as she'd done in the past. "I should add that you are a superior person in that you have demonstrated great kindness and compassion—and that has nothing to do with you being a duke. That, I think, is just who you are."

He stared at her. "That is one of the nicest things anyone has ever said to me." His voice was soft, almost disbelieving. It seemed he was also flattered.

Sadie was quite happy to participate in mutual admiration with him. It made her want to trust him completely. "I haven't even told you the worst part about what happened with Osborne."

His eyes rounded. "It gets worse?"

"I confronted him. I asked why he was ignoring me and if it was because I refused to let him take liberties with my person."

Lawford smiled at her in open admiration. "Of

course you did. What did the blackguard have to say for himself?"

The memory flashed in her mind—she didn't allow it much space, and it had been years since she'd even imagined his face, let alone that horrible encounter. "He laughed at me. I was so shocked that I just stood there while he turned and walked away. I asked some of the other girls who were also enjoying their first festival, and they—" Sadie's lungs hitched. She'd never told anyone this. She'd believed her emotions were long buried. Taking a breath, she steeled herself. "They also laughed. They said I shouldn't be so thin-skinned, that I ought to just have fun and stop being so serious. I felt so silly and naïve." She tipped her head down as her throat burned. She would not cry. Not four years later. Not in front of Law.

"Come with me." He started walking once more, pulling her along with him so that she had to move very fast to keep up. "We're going to the labyrinth, and we're going to banish that memory from your mind. We're going to replace it with something much better."

There were two ways to enter the labyrinth, which meant two separate paths to the center, which was a pond with ducks and a bridge leading to the other path so one could take another way out. Both labyrinthine paths included many alcoves, which were perfect spots for finding privacy. Sadie's heart crashed against her ribs as they approached the south entrance. What was he going to replace her terrible memory with?

"Is this the way you went in with that scoundrel?" Lawford asked.

"Yes, but this isn't really necessary. I rarely think of that anymore."

He escorted her into the labyrinth. The path

was wide enough for two couples to pass each other.

They reached the first alcove a moment later. These were narrow openings into slender spaces originally designed for one person to hide in, usually for the purposes of finding solitude. However, they were more often used for clandestine meetings.

"This one?" he asked.

Sadie pulled him to a stop. She looked up into his eyes. "This isn't necessary."

"I think it is. You may rarely think of it, but it clearly bothers you. You deserve nothing but happiness and a new memory to cherish instead of abhor."

"Then find a different alcove."

A few moments later, there was another alcove to the left. Lawford moved toward it, then immediately veered away. "Someone's in there," he whispered. He waggled his brows at her. "Wouldn't want to interrupt."

Putting her hand to her mouth to keep from giggling, Sadie grinned. At the third alcove, he approached slowly, then peered around the edge. Then he pulled her inside with him.

"This is rather snug," he said, rotating their positions so his back was to the opening. "Even more so than the cupboard this morning," he added in a husky murmur.

Their bodies were pressed together so that she could feel his heat and inhale his scent. Why had she wondered what he would replace her memory with? It seemed obvious. Still, she wanted to be sure.

"What did you have in mind to do here?"

He stroked his thumb along her chin and jaw.

"I'd thought to kiss you, but now I'm wondering if that will dredge up the bad memory."

She slid her hands up his coat and twined them around his neck. "I think you're right—this will give me a new memory. It's already much better than four years ago."

He chuckled softly. "I hope so." He looked into her eyes, his lips parted. She was desperate for him to put his mouth on hers.

"Kiss me, Law. Now."

Clasping her waist, he squeezed her just before his lips crashed onto hers. She wasn't sure what she'd expected, but heat and arousal immediately consumed her.

This wasn't how she'd ever expected a kiss to be. It completely overwhelmed her, but in the best way possible. It stirred some deep, dark passion she'd never known she had. She clutched at him, her lips and tongue tangling with his. His hands moved to her back and waist, at one point dipping to her backside and pulling her flush against his hips.

Desire pulsed within her, making her crave something beyond her reach. She knew enough of how bodies and sex worked to understand how to ease the occasional lustful ache, but Law's touch spun her to a new height, to a need that made her desperate for more.

His lips left hers, and he kissed along her cheek and jaw to her ear. "Is this better?" he whispered.

"Oh yes." She sucked in a breath as he licked and suckled her neck just beneath her ear. "But...I want more."

"Do you?" he murmured against her flesh. His hand came up and caressed her breast through her gown. "I confess I do too. The things I would like to do to you..."

"Tell me," she begged, spearing her hand into his thick hair.

He kissed the base of her throat, speaking between licks and gentle sucks. "I'd take your hair down so I could bury my face in it."

Her hair was thick, with coarse waves. "It's rather wild."

He lifted his head to look into her eyes. She could barely make his features out in the light from the lanterns spread along the labyrinth path. There was no mistaking the sensual smolder in his gaze, however. "I like wild."

He cupped her neck and put his thumb to her lips. "I'd strip your clothing away and I'd touch your breasts. I'd try a variety of things to arouse you. Hmm. I wonder which you would like best." He moved his hand down from her neck and tried to slide his fingers into her bodice. "This fits incredibly well. I'm afraid I can't touch you the way I'd like. Ah well, another time, perhaps." He kissed her again, making the thoughts in her head jumble within a delicious sensual haze.

Her breasts tingled, and she longed for him to touch her as he said. But he hadn't said. "How would you like to touch me?" she asked between kisses.

"I'd like to caress your breasts with extra attention for your nipples. Those are the most sensitive. I'd lick them and suck them, roll them between my fingers before I gave them a gentle pull."

Sadie dug her fingers into his scalp. "I want that."

"Alas, that would require disrupting your wardrobe in a way that we should not in our current situation."

"Then what else can you do?" She kissed him, long and deep, sliding her tongue along his as she'd learned to do in their short but wonderful acquaintance.

He lifted his head and gave her an earnest stare. "Do you really want to know?"

She nodded. "Please."

"I could...raise your gown so I may touch your sex. Is that what you want?"

"Yes." She'd denied the blackguard—whose name she couldn't even think of now, which made her positively elated—that very act. But with Law...she wanted that. She wanted *him*. "I want you to touch me. I want you to make me feel...complete."

He grinned before kissing her again, his teeth pulling on her lower lip before he moved down to her throat. "You want an orgasm?" he asked. "To come apart?"

Her body quivered in response. "Yes. Please."

He stripped the glove from his right hand and tucked it into his pocket. "You must be quiet, no matter what you feel. Can you do that?"

"Yes. Anything." She longed for him to deliver her from this torment while also relishing every moment.

Law bent and put his hand on her calf beneath her gown. Slowly, he skimmed his hand up her inner leg, eliciting shivers of desire that spread through her entire body. The skirt lifted with his hand as he kissed her neck.

Sadie cast her head back against the hedge, uncaring that it might pull at her hair. She could easily explain errant curls—for her, they were a when, not an if.

His hand cupped her sex, and she nearly collapsed as sensation cascaded through her. He stroked along her flesh, slowly at first, bringing his mouth back up to hers for a searing kiss.

Her hips bucked as he brushed the most sensitive part of her sex, the part she rubbed when she was trying to ease herself. Somehow, he was much better at it, sparking a continuous arc of pleasure and need. She wanted more. She wanted everything.

"Please, Law," she said against his mouth.

His finger slipped into her, and she would have cried out if he hadn't been kissing her. The intrusion was different, but felt so right. Her body welcomed him eagerly, her pelvis arching toward him. His movements were slow and deliberate, gradually gaining speed and friction. He alternated between using his finger to thrust into her and his hand to stroke her clitoris. It was soon a frenzy of motion, of utter rapture as her legs began to shake.

She felt the storm coming, the promise of absolute ecstasy. His hand moved ever faster driving her to the peak until she clenched around him, her muscles working to bring her to the climax.

Clutching at him, she gasped. It was too much. His hand closed over his mouth as he whispered, "Shhh," beside her ear. "Bite my hand if you must."

She would not. Could not. But she moaned as wave after wave of pleasure crashed over her. He didn't stop stroking her until the last shudder swept through her body.

After a final press of his palm over her sex, he pulled his hand away. Her gown fell back to her feet, and what was left of her quivered with a sublime satisfaction.

"Thank you," she rasped softly, her eyes closed as she leaned back against the hedge. She'd no idea she would feel so wonderful, so complete.

She opened her eyes to see him watching her, his eyes slitted, his jaw tight. "Are you all right?"

Exhaling through his nose, he nodded. "Yes."

His lips curled into a heart-stopping smile. "The only thing that matters, however, is that you are."

"More than," she said with a light chuckle. "I'm feeling rather scandalous, and even that is somehow lovely."

"You deserve to feel scandalous *and* lovely." He kissed her, then put his glove back on his hand. The hand that had, moments ago, given her an unrivaled pleasure. "Now, shall we walk to the center of the labyrinth so you can bask in your new memory?"

Sadie had never felt such gratitude and warmth for another person. How had this duke become such an integral part of her life in less than a week? "Yes, let's. There are a pair of follies at the center as well—one is a temple in its full glory, and the other is the same temple, but in ruins."

Law shook his head. "I can't imagine the thought and cost that went into these gardens."

"You can ask Phineas Radford about it tomorrow. His family owns and cares for the gardens—their estate borders the property. Someone from his family always judges the pudding competition, and he's been doing it the past few years."

They left the alcove, and Sadie wondered if her cheeks were aflame. She'd become quite heated during their...encounter. How was she walking through the labyrinth as if her life hadn't completely altered course just moments ago?

But had it, really? She was still Sadie Campion, unlikely maiden fair. In truth, she'd behaved even worse than four years ago. She'd allowed Law, a man to whom she was not betrothed and would not be betrothed, to touch her intimately.

Nevertheless, she couldn't bring herself to feel badly about it. She was glad for this year's festival, however it turned out. Now, she knew what she wanted. It was more than a yearning for a household and family of her own. She craved love and partnership, and she didn't want to settle for anything less.

He broke into her thoughts. "I want to apologize again for my attitude about wanting to strike gentlemen who wrong you. It's brutish and uncalled for."

"But what your father taught you, apparently." She understood what it was like to be raised in a certain manner, to develop behaviors that seemed inseparable from who you were. If her mother hadn't died and Sadie hadn't taken on responsibility at a young age, how different might she be?

"Yes." Law was quiet a moment as they passed another couple on their way toward the center. "In the months since he died, I've realized I don't want to be like him. And now, without him scrutinizing my every move, I don't have to be."

"He sounds demanding."

"Very. That's not to say he was cruel or overly harsh. He laughed all the time. But he wasn't kind or generous. He needed to be at the center of everything—adored and admired."

"Is that what you want?" She felt him shudder in response.

"God, no. In his shadow, I wanted to disappear. The comparisons between us were inevitable, and I was always found lacking."

"What of your mother?"

"I think I told you that she died when I was fourteen. She'd given birth to her eighth child, and it was all her body could take."

Sadie turned her head toward him as she clutched his arm more tightly. "But you only have two younger sisters."

"The others didn't survive. She lost some before

it was time for them to be born. The others died shortly after entering the world. My father was devastated that she couldn't give him a spare. Yet, he didn't remarry after she was gone. I think he truly loved her."

"That's something, I suppose."

"I don't really know since he never told me." He gave her a faint smile. "Perhaps it's just more comforting if I imagine it that way."

His words went straight to her heart. Sadie knew what it was like to make excuses for a parent who wasn't always as supportive or aware as they ought to be. "Were you and your sisters close?"

"As much as we could be. They are five and seven years younger than I am. They share a strong sisterly bond that is much different from what I share with them. That makes me happy. I looked out for them, and it was important to me that they marry well." He chuckled. "That's the name of your town."

She smiled. "Yes, and I've never truly considered what that means." They turned a corner, moving closer to the center. "Marrying well, I mean."

"That they wed someone appropriate, but mostly that they are happy. My youngest sister married one of my friends from Oxford. He doesn't have a title—he's the grandson of an earl. My father was not in favor of the marriage, but I convinced him to accept what my sister wanted. I knew they would be happy together, and they are."

She heard the love in his voice and thought his sisters were incredibly lucky to have him. However, it also made her feel a bit...bad about her own brothers. Would they want the same for her? They were certainly enthusiastic about a potential match with Law, but that had come from before they—or she—had even come to know him.

"I'm so glad for her," Sadie said. "But I'm sorry your father couldn't embrace your sister's choice. Was that because he wasn't titled?"

"Yes, and, in my father's opinion, he lacked the ability to be as forceful and…dominating as he should be. He had high expectations for me and my sisters. He wasn't entirely in the wrong. There are standards to being a duke, or at least a great deal of responsibility and duty. I take my role in the House of Lords very seriously, probably more seriously than my father did. He liked wielding power. I do too, but for the purpose of effecting change."

Everything he said only made her appreciate him more. If she wasn't careful, she thought she could love him. If she didn't already.

No, no. She couldn't allow that. The chasm between them was insurmountable. Just listening to him talk about his responsibilities was enough to make her recognize they had no future together, no matter how much they enjoyed each other's company. He led a complicated life in the heart of Society, and she made sure the larder was stocked and that everyone had clean linens. She'd no idea how to support him in London, and she had to think her naïveté would lead her to humiliation and failure.

They'd reached the center of the labyrinth, a wide space of a few acres. Dozens of people were gathered, and right away, a couple came toward them.

Law had certainly accomplished what he'd set out to do: the labyrinth was no longer a place that gave her anxiety and made her feel foolish. Instead, it was a place of magic and wonder, where she'd connected in the most intimate way—both physically and emotionally—with Law. It was, perhaps, the place where she'd fallen in love.

It was also where she realized that love could not flourish. Unless...there really was such a thing as magic. Because that was the only way she'd ever be a duchess.

CHAPTER 10

Law had watched Sadie dance with a few men after they'd left the labyrinth. One was the gentleman with whom she'd danced earlier in the evening. Of all the men she interacted with, she seemed to smile and laugh the most with him. Perhaps he would offer for her.

The thought provoked a powerful jealousy in Law.

They'd arranged to meet at the gate at midnight in order to return to Fieldstone. Now, as Law drove them back to her home, he hoped she might fall asleep on his shoulder again. Anything to have her near.

His mind was full of their encounter in the labyrinth. That she'd trusted him in the place where another man had so utterly failed her filled him with a wonder and joy he'd never experienced. She made him feel things he'd never imagined, and the prospect of losing that was beginning to be more than he could bear.

Beside him, Sadie yawned. "Pardon me," she said after lowering her hand from her mouth. "I'm not sure which is harder work—managing Fieldstone or being a maiden fair."

Law chuckled. "Which do you enjoy more?"

"Managing Fieldstone," she responded without hesitation. "It happens that I am a simple woman at heart."

He'd known that about her, could see that the happiness she hunted would have to include the things that gave her purpose and defined her self-worth: hard work, loyalty, helping others, and much more. This was just one of many things about her that he found so compelling.

"Sadie, I want you to know that I don't take what happened in the labyrinth lightly. I've come to care for you a great deal." He slid his gaze toward her to see her looking at him.

Her smile was warm and familiar—Law could never tire of seeing that, especially when it was directed at him. "That's lovely to hear. I care for you as well. And I have no regrets about what happened."

"I'm glad." Law needed to open himself to her completely. He could no longer hide what he'd been on his way to do when fate had delivered him to Sadie's doorstep. "I hope you'll continue to feel positively toward me after I confess something that I should have told you from the start."

Her smile faded. "What's that?"

Taking a deep breath, Law plowed forward. "I was on my way to Dorset when the wheel came off my coach. Before my father died, he asked me to—no, he demanded that I wed his friend's daughter. I said I would consider it, but he wrote to Lord Gillingham before he died and told him that the betrothal between me and his daughter was imminent. I put Gillingham off for six months, but I was finally on my way to meet his daughter. If we suited, we would sign a marriage contract."

Law stole a glance at her. Her focus was on the

road before them, her features impassive. It was a long moment before she finally spoke.

Turning her head toward him, she asked, "Why didn't you just say all that when you arrived?"

"I didn't want to think of it, let alone discuss it. I'd already been having second thoughts. I saw the accident as a reprieve from a future I wasn't sure I wanted." He should not have told her this while driving. He wanted to take her hands, to hold her, to look into her eyes. "Every hour and day I spend here with you is confirmation of that—I don't want to marry Lady Frederica. I don't even care to meet her. She represents my father's expectations, which I have long tried to fulfill, to my own displeasure. I've come to realize that I want to be my own man, make my own choices. I don't want to spare a thought as to what my father would want or think."

"I sensed your relationship with your father was poor, but now I see it was more complicated than that."

"I don't want it to be. Not anymore. I want to be free of him. I am not interested in being the most admired or feared man in the room, nor do I need to command everyone's attention with arrogance and might. You say you're a simple woman, and I suppose I've learned that I'd like to be a simpler man."

"Is that possible for a duke?"

Law laughed. "I'll let you know."

She fell silent again, and he had to work to hold his tongue, to let her consider and respond in her own time.

As they neared the drive to Fieldstone, she said, "Is there anything else you're hiding from me?"

The note of distrust in her voice tore at him. "No, there isn't anything else. I should like very much to send word to Lord Gillingham that I won't be coming, but I will have to wait until after the festival to find someone to take a message to Dorset."

"Yes, although if you truly wanted to send one now, you could find somebody equal to the task—for an exorbitant fee."

"Honestly, I'd rather not be the reason someone misses the festival. I've become wholly invested now." He turned onto the drive toward the house.

She smiled at him. "Marrywell has a way of winning people over."

"Marrywell certainly helped, but you're the reason I'm invested, the reason I don't want to leave, the reason I'm not marrying Lady Frederica or anyone else." He heard her intake of breath and silently cursed the fact that he couldn't take her in his arms.

Thankfully, they reached the house a moment later, and he stopped the gig in front. Bryan was waiting for them and took the reins as Law climbed down. "Thank you, Bryan," he murmured before circling around to Sadie.

She took his hand, and he grinned with the joy of touching her. He helped her down, and they stood for a moment looking into each other's eyes.

"Night, then," Bryan said before driving toward the stables.

"We should go inside," Sadie said softly.

"In a moment," Law whispered. He removed his glove from his right hand and caressed her face. "I'm so sorry I didn't tell you about the purpose of my journey. I didn't mean to hide it from you. *I* was hiding from it."

"I know what it's like to hide. That's what I've been doing the past four years since Osborne made me feel so ridiculous. It was much easier to immerse myself in my work here at Fieldstone, where I feel competent and worthwhile."

He stroked her jaw with his thumb. "I hate that you ever felt you weren't, even for a moment. I don't want you to hide anymore. You deserve the future you want—a house and a family." He hesitated, but only the barest moment. "Are three houses too many?"

Her eyes rounded. "You aren't suggesting—"

"I am asking." Law smiled, never more sure of anything in his life. "Could you find a way to be my duchess? To share my life, my home—homes—and be my family?"

She blinked several times. "Law, I never imagined—" She pressed her fingers to her mouth as her eyes glimmered in the light from the lantern next to the door. Lowering her hand, she took a breath. "I'm the daughter of a farmer. You're a duke. I don't know how this would work."

"I know it would be an adjustment. I will be right by your side every step of the way. It's a great deal to ask—leaving Marrywell, though we'd visit as often as you like. I really do love it here."

Her brow furrowed, and her distress was evident. "I don't know. I need to think."

Law leaned forward and kissed her forehead, then her cheek. Then he lightly brushed his lips against hers. "Take as much time as you need. I'm not going anywhere. Unless you ask me to." He felt her shiver. "Let's get you inside."

Putting his hand on her lower back, he guided her into the house. "Should I extinguish the lantern?" Law asked.

"No, Bryan will come back and do it once he's sure everyone has returned."

They walked upstairs together. Law kept glancing over at her. Her jaw was tight, her features tense. He worried she was angry with him for not telling her about his potential betrothal.

Outside their rooms, she turned to him. Law realized he'd been holding his breath since the stairs.

"I want to say yes," she said.

Though he heard the hesitation in her voice, Law couldn't help the joy that surged inside him. "Then say yes."

She laughed softly. "I wish it were that easy. And yet...perhaps it is. I do care for you. I just...it would be a very big change for me."

"I understand. Take some time to consider it. Please." He ought to tell her that he loved her—because he did. But he'd already shocked her—and himself—with his proposal. He'd wait to tell her until tomorrow. "May I kiss you?"

She slipped her hand back to cradle his neck. "Always."

Wrapping his arms around her, he pulled her against him as his lips met hers. There was heat and reverence and a crushing need to claim her as his. But he would be patient.

Her tongue met his, and he eagerly swept into her mouth, losing himself in her lush abandon. Her fingers speared through the hair at his nape, urging him to deepen the kiss. Law angled his head and caressed her back, her waist, her backside. She pressed her pelvis to his, and Law was all too aware of his stiff cock, already desperate from their earlier activities in the labyrinth.

Law lifted his head, panting, and took a step back. "We should go to bed."

She arched a brow at him in the most flirtatious expression he'd ever seen on her face. He laughed. "I meant separately."

"Well, that is probably for the best." She

sounded disappointed, and that gave him hope. "I don't know if I'll be able to sleep."

"Let me know if you can't." He winked at her. "Good night, Sadie."

"Good night, Law." She turned and went to open her door. Before stepping inside, she looked back at him over her shoulder. "I'll try to have an answer for you in the morning."

"I meant what I said. Take as much time as you need."

She gave him a slight nod, then closed the door.

Law turned to go into his room just as Yates was coming down the corridor. Dammit, he'd been so caught up with Sadie that he hadn't even thought of the valet coming to prepare him for bed. Had Yates seen them kissing?

"I saw that you arrived," Yates said in a clipped tone, his expression sour, but then it often was.

If he'd seen them in the drive, then he'd likely witnessed their near embrace if not their kiss of a moment ago. Law narrowed his eyes at Yates. "Keep any commentary to yourself. I'm not interested in hearing it."

"I suppose a dalliance before you wed is to be expected," Yates said as he opened the door for Law. "Your father would not have begrudged you that."

Law snapped his head toward the valet. "Miss Campion is not a dalliance. That is commentary, and I told you I didn't want to hear it. Furthermore, I don't care to hear my father's opinion. I realize you feel a certain loyalty to him, but I am my own man."

"Of course you are, Your Grace. I am merely offering your father's voice since he is no longer here. He wanted me to guide you, and since you took me on as your valet, I thought you wanted that too."

Damn. Now Law felt somewhat badly about being curt. He exhaled, letting out his frustration. "I appreciate what you're trying to do. However, it is time for me to stand on my own—without my father's counsel. Can you understand that?"

Yates inclined his head in response. "I suppose I can."

"Good." Law went into the chamber. Then he turned and blocked the doorway before Yates could follow him. "I don't require your assistance this evening. You may retire." Law preferred to be alone in order to contemplate how he might woo Sadie into accepting his proposal.

Bowing, Yates said, "Good evening," before closing the door. Law heard him walk away.

Dismissing the valet from his mind, Law stripped away his coat and focused on a far more tantalizing prospect—Sadie as his duchess. Though his proposal hadn't been planned, he didn't regret making it for one moment. He just hoped she'd say yes.

~

Sadie had no idea how long she lay in bed staring at the ceiling. It wasn't just her mind churning with Law's surprising proposal; it was also her body yearning for his touch. She'd been so close to inviting him into her bedchamber so they could finish what they'd started in the labyrinth.

When she thought of how he'd brought her such rapture, she wondered why she hadn't immediately said yes to his proposal. But it was more than that. He was also kind, charming, and protective in a way that made her feel like she was the most special person in the world—at least to him. And that was what mattered, wasn't it?

That he'd helped her this week meant more to her than she could say. He'd promised to see her betrothed, and here she was at the end of day five and she could very well be...

She bolted upright. Was that why he'd proposed?

Throwing the coverlet off, Sadie jumped from the bed. She didn't bother to don slippers or a dressing gown before hurrying from her chamber. Closing her door, she moved over to his. Then she hesitated. Should she knock?

No, she didn't want to wake anyone else.

She pushed open the door and stepped inside. The only light was the coals in the hearth, but it was enough to make out Law's form on the bed. She moved toward him and stopped short as she realized he was...nude.

"Sadie!" He dove under the covers and pulled them up to his waist. "I didn't hear you come in."

"My apologies. I..." Her mouth had gone dry. She hadn't seen exactly what he'd been doing, but she'd heard him breathing—rapidly—and seen his hand moving in the vicinity of his pelvis. "I needed to speak with you. I should have knocked, but I didn't want to wake anyone. I didn't mean to, ah, interrupt you."

"Come closer." He waited until she moved to the side of the bed. "Did you see what I was doing?"

"Not entirely, but I could, ah, guess."

"You know what men do to pleasure themselves?"

"I have four brothers. Sometimes they say things when they don't think I'm listening—or they don't realize I'm in the room and can hear them talking."

"I see," Law murmured. His breathing had slowed to normal. "I hope that wasn't shocking. Hearing them talk or seeing me engaged in…it."

"I didn't see much, but I confess I'm now intrigued."

He grunted softly. "For the love of God, Sadie, why are you here?" The question was practically a growl. It wasn't a fearsome sound, but a…seductive one.

"Why are you asking like that?"

"Because I am desperate for release, and your being intrigued by my frigging myself has got to be the single most erotic thing I've heard."

Frigging…yes, that was a word she'd heard before. And she certainly knew what it felt like to want release. "It feels good?" She assumed it must.

"It satisfies a need. It would feel much better if you did it or if…never mind." He sounded as if he couldn't breathe.

"Could I help you finish, then?" she asked. "I should like to return the favor you gave me in the labyrinth."

Law groaned. The sound was dark and seductive. It stirred Sadie's desire, which she realized had sparked as soon as she'd learned what he was doing to himself.

"You still didn't answer why you are here." He still sounded strained, as if he were in pain.

"It's silly, probably. I wondered if you'd proposed in order to fulfill your promise that you'd see me betrothed by the end of the festival."

"Sadie." He said her name like a plea, low and rough, as if he might perish if he couldn't have… something. He moved on the bed, pushing the covers back as he reached for her.

Sweeping her up, he laid her on the mattress, then hovered over her before setting one knee between her legs. "Sadie," he repeated, but softer. "That is *not* why I proposed to you. I want you to be my duchess because I love you. Because when I think of leaving Marrywell and never seeing you again, I'm filled with a terrible anguish."

He loved her? She'd suspected she felt the same, but she hadn't allowed herself to let it be true. But hearing him say it and seeing the emotion in his gaze, she felt the same emotion unfurl inside her. "I love you too." Suddenly the divide between them didn't seem so vast. It would be a monumental change, and she might very well falter, but he would be at her side. Love had seemed a luxury, but now that it was here staring her in the face, she didn't want to turn away. "Yes, I'll marry you."

She put her hands on his shoulders and ran her fingertips along his collarbones. Then she dragged them down to his chest until she reached his nipples. He sucked in a breath, and she smiled at his reaction.

"Did you really say yes?" he whispered.

She nodded. "I did. And now, I want you to let me help you finish. You said I could do it for you." She moved one hand down to his abdomen. His breathing grew more rapid, sounding nearly like when she'd first come in. "Or there was something else—did you mean that you could finish inside me?"

He kissed her then, his mouth claiming hers with a ravenous passion that set her completely aflame. His tongue thrust into her, sliding along hers with a dominance and desperation she felt in her soul. She gripped his hip as he caressed her breast through the linen of her night rail.

Tearing his lips from hers, he kissed down her

throat, licking her flesh. He pulled at her bodice, widening the drawstring so that he could tug the garment down to expose her breasts.

"You are magnificent." He used his thumb to tweak her nipple, sending shocks of need straight to her sex. His hand cupped her as he licked her cleavage.

"They're too big."

"They are not. They are glorious." He moved his mouth over the globe he held, then closed his lips around her nipple. He licked and sucked, drawing on her flesh until she cried out.

His other hand moved to the other breast, caressing and stroking until she was arching her back and whimpering for more. He pinched the nipple as he suckled the other. Sadie had no idea such pleasure could come from this.

She thrust her fingers into his hair, clutching his head as she writhed beneath him. "I was supposed to be helping you," she managed to say.

"You *are* helping me. This is everything I've ever dreamed of. Almost." He pushed up the hem of her night rail, then lifted his head so he could remove the garment from her entirely.

When she lay naked beneath him, he stared at her body. "You are absolutely beautiful." He cupped her breasts, pushing them together. "Not too big. Perfect." He closed his fingers and thumbs around her nipples, tugging on them until she begged him to…she didn't know what.

"Please, Law, I need you."

He suckled her again, first one breast then the other, taking long minutes to savor her flesh. She quivered as her body reached new heights of arousal. Her sex felt heavy and wet. If he didn't touch her there soon, she might weep.

He kissed along her abdomen, licking lower

until he reached her sex. Putting one hand beneath her backside, he told her to spread her legs wider.

"What are you doing?" She looked down at his head between her thighs.

His gaze met hers as he lifted her from the mattress. "You said you needed me. Here I am." Then his mouth was on her sex, his tongue licking her folds and that spot at the top that had given her such pleasure earlier.

He clutched her backside, holding her as a feast for his mouth. His tongue thrust into her, and she gripped his head, her fingers tangling in his hair. Her hips moved as she sought more of him.

His lips and tongue moved greedily over and into her sex, working her into a frenzy of need. When he stroked the top of her sex, every muscle in her body clenched as she rushed toward release. At last, she saw the light—its heat and wonder enveloping her in an exquisite rapture. Her body went stiff as she catapulted into her climax.

~

Law watched Sadie bask in ecstasy, her head cast back, her lips parted as she whimpered and moaned. Her legs quivered around him as her orgasm began to fade. He kissed her thigh before rising over her.

Her eyes fluttered open. "That was somehow even better than the labyrinth."

"I should hope so. We have the benefit of time and comfort here," he said with a wicked grin.

She narrowed her eyes at him. "Now, are you going to finish?"

"If you'll allow it."

"I'm going to demand it," she said, echoing her words before their first kiss.

"You are a demanding, domineering woman," he mused. "I like that."

"Good. I wish to touch your…cock. That's the best word, I think."

"The best word…of all the words?" he asked with a laugh.

"Of words I have heard in reference to your sex."

"Ah, yes, brothers." He took her hand and curled it around his shaft. His eyes closed briefly as he surrendered to the sheer pleasure of her touch. Then she gripped him, and he feared he would spend into her hand. He moaned, unable to stop himself from thrusting his hips to slide across her palm.

"You could finish like this?" she asked as she continued to stroke him. He was helping her but realized she didn't need his assistance.

"I could, but I'd rather come inside you. Unless you'd prefer to wait to do that." He met her gaze, breathless for her response. Either was a gift he hadn't expected tonight.

"I think I'd like to feel you inside me. Show me what to do." Her words were a command, and he loved her sense of authority. How could she continue to become even more perfect?

He positioned his hips against hers and stroked her sex. She was wet again already. "We're going to guide me to your sheath."

She didn't need the direction as she was lifting her hips and seeking his entry. He slid the tip into her and drove slowly forward. She tilted her pelvis, and he wrapped one of her legs around his hip. She immediately did the same with the other, and he was soon fully seated within her.

"All right?" he asked before kissing her temple, her jaw, her neck.

"Yes."

He brushed his lips across hers, but she gripped his head and held him so she could deepen the kiss. She speared her tongue into his mouth, and he eagerly met her.

She wiggled her hips, prompting him to move. God, he wasn't sure how long he was going to last. He couldn't recall ever being so aroused.

He thrust slowly at first, wanting to give her time to adjust to this newness. Her heels dug into his backside as she rotated her pelvis against his, her body straining to receive him. She was so bloody eager and honest in her desire, but then he expected nothing less from this remarkable woman.

His balls began to tighten as blood rushed to his cock. He had to go faster. "Come with me, Sadie," he said as he tangled his hand in the waves of her hair and pumped into her.

"Yes, Law. That feels so good. How does that feel so good?"

He smiled at her sense of wonder, but only for a moment before his body demanded his full attention. He snapped his hips against hers, driving hard and deep. His body began to tighten as his orgasm neared. He felt her clench around him and slipped his hand between them to stroke her clitoris. She moaned his name as her legs squeezed him.

He came in a blinding flash and had to clamp his jaw together to keep from shouting the house down as rapture claimed him. He continued thrusting, carrying them both into the darkness and on to ecstasy. When he glimpsed the light once more, he was finally spent.

Law settled to the side of her, not wanting to crush her with his weight.

"Where did you go?" she asked softly, her

breath coming in rapid pants.

"I'm just here." He pressed his lips to her cheek.

"I liked you on top of me. You could have stayed there. At least for a moment."

"I'll keep that in mind for next time," he said, smiling.

"Next time… When will that be, I wonder? After we're married?"

"Perhaps, unless we can manage to steal moments like this." Law nuzzled her neck. He heard her yawn. "Let me walk you back to your room. It's probably not wise for us to fall asleep."

"No, we shouldn't chance being caught—even though we are…betrothed." She said the last word with a note of uncertainty.

Law rose up beside her and looked down into her face. He stroked her temple and cheek before caressing her head so he could feel her soft curls. He loved seeing them unbound. "I hope you don't regret accepting my proposal."

"It's just surprising. I need time to acclimate my mind."

"I understand." He kissed her, his lips lingering against hers. He didn't want to let her go, but he must. "Come, let's get you back to your own bed."

"I can walk across the corridor," she said with a light laugh.

"I'm still going to escort you."

She grinned at him as he handed her the discarded night rail. "You are as committed and loyal as any knight."

He slipped from the bed and gave her a courtly bow. "It is my honor." Moving to find his dressing gown, he marveled at how much his life had changed in less than a week. He never could have dreamed he would find this measure of happiness.

He couldn't wait to share it with his wife.

CHAPTER 11

Law had awakened the following morning with a smile that he'd felt certain he'd worn since he'd walked Sadie back to her room. He'd slept remarkably well. They only thing that would have made it better would have been if Sadie had remained with him.

He was still in awe of where he found himself today—as a betrothed man anticipating his marriage. Just a week ago, he'd been dreading this state, but then this was an entirely different woman, a wholly unexpected and welcome change of plans.

He needed to write to Gillingham to inform him that he wouldn't be marrying his daughter. Law felt bad about potentially disappointing Lady Frederica, but perhaps she would be as relieved as he'd felt when he'd learned his trip would be delayed. It wasn't as if they shared affection. They hadn't even met. Still, he would write the letter in such a way as to ensure she understood this was nothing to do with her personally. Law was simply already in love with someone else and, happily, she'd consented to be his wife.

Bryan had returned from driving Sadie into

town and was now providing the same service for Law. When they reached the assembly rooms, Law thanked the lad and whistled on his way inside.

He hadn't even realized he *could* whistle.

A young man of perhaps fourteen or fifteen met him just after he entered. "Welcome, Your Grace. I'm Bertrand. I'll take you to the judging area."

"Thank you, Bertrand." Law followed the boy into the ballroom, where tables had been set up in rows. They were laden with dishes, and a handful of ladies were setting up little signs, presumably indicating what the puddings were.

"The judges are just over here, waiting for Mrs. Armstrong to explain how everything works," Bertrand said, gesturing to an area to the side of the dais.

Nodding, Law made his way to where six or seven other people were sitting. Except for one fellow, who was standing. A tall man with broad shoulders, he looked to be a few years younger than Law's twenty-nine. His dark auburn hair was a touch on the long side, and his clothing wasn't the latest style, but it was well tailored and made of fine materials.

"You must be the Duke of Lawford," the man said, inclining his head. "I'm Phineas Radford." He held out his hand, and Law shook it.

"The gentleman who oversees the botanical gardens? They are an astonishing achievement. I can't imagine what that cost. Or what it continues to cost you."

The younger man's features tightened—it wasn't quite a grimace, but it might have been if Radford had allowed it. "Yes, my family cultivated the botanical gardens and donated the land for the town's use right about the time the matchmaking festival was reborn nearly fifty years ago."

"Everything is so well maintained. You must employ a great many gardeners and the like."

"Probably fewer than you would think," he said drily. "I understand this is your first time at the festival? And that you hadn't even intended to come?"

It seemed everyone knew Law's precise circumstances. Well, not *precise*, since no one knew he was supposed to be finalizing his betrothal somewhere else. "Yes, that's correct. I've found it surprisingly delightful."

"You're staying at Fieldstone? I imagine Sadie is taking good care of you."

Law swallowed his immediate response to that, which was to say, yes, she was taking very good care of him and he was over the moon. Instead, he noted that Radford called her Sadie, and that he'd mentioned her and not anyone else at Fieldstone. He was likely aware that she was in charge there. Did everyone know that? Honestly, why wouldn't they?

"Indeed she is," Law replied. "She takes very good care of everyone. I do wonder why her father hasn't remarried when his town holds an annual matchmaking festival."

Radford chuckled. "Don't think plenty of women haven't tried, though I think they gave up a few years back."

Was Campion not interested in taking another wife? "He could at least hire a housekeeper," Law muttered.

"What's that?" Radford asked, leaning closer. "They hired a housekeeper? What an astounding development! I don't mind saying it's past time." He wrinkled his nose slightly. "Forget I said that, please. It isn't my place to comment on another's household."

"Already forgotten," Law said, though he would

recall every detail of this informative conversation. "But to answer your question, no, they have not hired a housekeeper. I was saying Campion should—to relieve his daughter's burden."

Radford's hazel eyes glinted. "He may have to if she accepts a proposal tomorrow."

Law had to bite the inside of his cheek to keep from blurting out that she already had. Thankfully, Mrs. Armstrong arrived just then and explained their duties.

They were to visit each table and sample the puddings in that category. They would choose their top three favorites, ranking them first, second, and third. Then the votes would be tallied and winners in each category would be chosen. They must also choose a best overall pudding after they had sampled everything.

Looking at the quantity of puddings, Law began to regret agreeing to this task. "Pardon me, Mrs. Armstrong, are we all judging every pudding? I don't think I have the fortitude."

She laughed. "Goodness no, Your Grace! We have you divided up so that you'll taste five or six categories. Don't fret, some of them only have two puddings."

"Here come the maidens fair," Radford said. "Sadie looks very pretty. I was so happy when the queen chose her as an eighth maiden. She's been overlooked for far too long."

Yes, she had. Law watched her file in—at the end of the line—her light brown hair wound atop her head in a braided style and crowned with blue and white flowers. They complemented her blue walking dress. Her gaze met Law's as she walked past him and gave him a smile that heated his body.

As the maidens moved onto the dais, Radford jabbed his elbow into Law's side. "Any chance you might be the one to propose to Sadie? The odds are favoring that outcome, if you care about that sort of thing."

Law turned his head to look at Radford. "There are wagers as to what matches are made?"

"Of course. The primary betting book is at the Wheatsheaf."

Marrywell was perhaps more like London than one might anticipate.

As he sampled puddings, his gaze kept drifting to Sadie on the dais. She chatted occasionally with the maiden next to her, but was mostly quiet with her hands folded in her lap.

Law passed Radford as he moved to the next table. "Why don't the maidens judge?"

"They used to until one became very ill." He made a face. "She ate a little too much pudding. After that, none of the maidens wanted to shoulder the responsibility. So, they sit on the dais and watch. Boring as hell, if you ask me."

"I was thinking the same thing. They should at least be allowed to sample the pudding." Law would recommend a few of his favorites to Sadie. There was an absolutely sublime bread and butter pudding that was, so far, his choice for best of the lot.

People came in and out of the ballroom, but a group of ladies at the back of the room watched the entire proceedings. Law had to think they were the cooks, particularly since Mrs. Rowell was among them. Had she made the bread and butter pudding he liked so well? He wouldn't be surprised.

"Lawford!"

Law had just picked up a fork at the Bakewell pudding table, which was directly in front of the dais, when he heard his name from behind him.

Turning, he nearly dropped the fork. Coming straight toward him was Lord bloody Gillingham.

Two ladies followed behind him, one whose age indicated she was likely Lady Gillingham, and a young lady with pale blonde hair and wide blue eyes. She looked rather like a doll, which was precisely how Law's father had described her.

Bloody hell.

Before Law could suggest they step outside, Gillingham gave him a jovial smile. "There he is! You look well, Lawford, despite what you've endured." Short of stature, Gillingham had a hooked nose and sculpted, austere features. His hair was still a dark sable, though it had turned gray at the temples. "Allow me to present my daughter, Lady Frederica, your dear betrothed." He spoke loudly and clearly. Everyone in the room would have heard him.

Law darted a look at Sadie on the dais. She was watching the scene unfold, her eyes wide. Indeed, all the maidens were fixed on Law and the new arrivals.

Keeping his voice low, Law moved closer to Gillingham. He didn't wish to make more of a scene than the earl's arrival already had. "You are mistaken. There is no betrothal." At least not one including Lady Frederica.

Gillingham's thick, dark brows drew together. "Perhaps not yet, at least not officially. But as you said in your letter, it's as good as done."

"My what?" Law's heart pounded.

"The letter you sent," Lady Frederica responded. She'd stepped toward them and took a piece of folded parchment from her reticule. "It was so charming. I've been eager to meet you too." She gave him a tentative smile.

Who in the bloody hell had sent them a letter

pretending to be him? "May I see that?" He took the letter from Lady Frederica and unfolded it. The handwriting wasn't his, of course, and though he wasn't completely certain, he suspected it belonged to Yates. Law transferred his gaze to the earl as he clenched his jaw. "May we go outside to continue this conversation?"

Mrs. Sneed and Mrs. Armstrong joined them, preventing Gillingham's response.

"May I be of help?" Mrs. Sneed asked pertly, her gaze hungry for information—or more accurately, gossip.

"No, thank you," Law said smoothly. The woman swept her attention over the Gillinghams. Law wasn't going to be able to avoid introducing them. Unless he wanted to follow his father's direction and simply do as he pleased. Law could hear him now: *"Fuck the rules!"* That didn't apply to when he expected Law to follow them, of course.

However, Law was not his overbearing father nor did he want to be. He was overcome with the need to be as different from him as possible, to separate himself from his father's demands and expectations.

He introduced the two women based on their rank in the town. "Lord Gillingham, allow me to present Mrs. Armstrong, whose husband is the mayor of Marrywell, and Mrs. Sneed, whose husband is the constable."

Lord Gillingham introduced his wife and daughter. Lady Frederica kept darting disappointed looks at Law. She did indeed look like a doll—one that might break.

Law glanced toward the dais once more, and his heart sank. Sadie stared straight ahead, her face pale, her back stiff. Now *she* looked as though she might break, and it would be entirely his fault.

"Welcome to the Marrywell May Day Matchmaking Festival!" Mrs. Sneed said. "You're rather late, but no matter. We've plenty of activities going on across the street at the botanical gardens as well as the market fair along the High Street, but I'm sure you saw that as you drove in. Tonight, there will be more dancing, as well as a hide-and-seek game in the labyrinth. It will be such fun, particularly if there's a betrothal we can announce this evening." She looked expectantly between Gillingham and Law.

Law opened his mouth to refute the idea of a betrothal, but Lady Gillingham cut him off. "That sounds delightfully amusing. We came here straightaway in order for my daughter to greet her betrothed—they are most eager to be wed—so we still need to secure lodging. Where do you recommend?"

Mrs. Sneed and Mrs. Armstrong exchanged looks of sympathy, then directed them at Lady Gillingham. Mrs. Sneed said, "There isn't anywhere to lodge, I'm afraid. However, you're more than welcome to stay with us. We've plenty of room."

Mrs. Armstrong clapped her hands together. "A ducal betrothal. I can't recall the last time that happened at our festival!"

"I daresay they'll be voted next year's king and queen," Mrs. Sneed said.

"I thought the duke was courting Sadie." This came from one of the maidens fair.

Everyone's attention swung toward the dais.

"Who's Sadie?" Gillingham asked. "Sounds like a name for a cow."

Lady Gillingham tittered. "Can you imagine the Duke of Lawford courting someone so beneath him? The mere idea is ridiculous." She laughed brightly, waving her hand, and her husband and daughter joined in. Both Mrs. Sneed and Mrs. Armstrong smiled, but they looked slightly uncomfortable. Two of the maidens fair also laughed, and there were a few chuckles around the room. Law seethed at anyone who would find humor in the Gillinghams' cruel mockery.

"Enough!" Law brandished the letter. "I didn't write this. I do not plan to wed Lady Frederica."

Lady Frederica's face fell, and she sucked in her lower lip, snagging it between her teeth. "You aren't looking forward to marrying me?"

Law was angry that she'd laughed at Sadie, but he still hated the hurt in her eyes. "I'm afraid not." He was going to skewer Yates for causing this poor girl torment.

Except hadn't Law also caused it, at least in part? He hadn't promised to marry her, but he *had* agreed to see if they would suit. Now, he wasn't even going to do that much. How could he when he was already so desperately in love with Sadie?

Gillingham's lip curled. "You can't renege on your promise."

Law crumpled the letter. "I never made a promise."

"Your father did, and it's up to you to honor it!" Gillingham's nostrils flared.

"There is no formal agreement, nothing binding," Law insisted. "I realize it's disappointing, and I'm sorry."

"You think you can just pretend there was no agreement, but I know better. Most of London knows better. Your match with Frederica has been talked about for weeks."

Law hadn't been aware of that and wasn't sure he believed it. "That changes nothing. You can't force me to wed your daughter." Dammit, he still felt horrible for Lady Frederica. Law turned to her and gentled his tone. "I'm very sorry about this and how it may affect you. But I simply can't marry you."

"I'd heard you might be a scoundrel," Lady Frederica said. "Now I know for certain that you are. I'll be ruined."

Though Law didn't want that to be true, he knew Society could be vicious. He tried to reassure her. "Nonsense. Your father is a wealthy earl. You'll make an excellent match."

Lady Frederica sniffed and blinked. Was she fighting off tears? "*You* are an excellent match."

Lady Gillingham put her arm around her daughter. She scowled at Law. "Your father would be horrified by your behavior. The gossip this will cause will follow us all for months or longer. Perhaps forever. Shame on you!"

For years, Law had succumbed to his father's demands. It was easier than resisting him, and after his mother's death, he'd hoped to please his father in some small way, to see him be happy if only for a moment. Now that he was gone, Law didn't have to do that anymore. He wasn't going to submit to what his father had promised, and he certainly wasn't going to let Yates, his father's emissary, it seemed, manipulate him into doing so.

"*I'm* horrified that you misinterpreted my intent and that my valet saw fit to mislead you with this forged letter. I'm deeply sorry for any hurt or embarrassment this may cause to Lady Frederica, but I doubt she would want to marry me knowing I love someone else." He glanced toward the dais, but Sadie's chair was empty. When had she gone? Dammit! He longed to race after her, but he needed to settle this.

"I will gladly shoulder any blame for the lack of

a betrothal between us, but this is the end of things. If you'll excuse me." He started to move past them, but Gillingham grabbed his elbow.

"You're worse than a scoundrel. I can't imagine you'll be happy with some provincial chit."

Law resisted the urge to punch the man for referring to Sadie in that manner. But she *was* provincial, and he loved that about her. "I'll be more than happy. I'll be the luckiest man in the world," Law said softly. "While you will be bitter and cruel. Your belittlement of a perfectly lovely young woman today was an appalling embarrassment. You're the one who should be ashamed." He flicked a glance toward Lady Gillingham to include her in that assessment.

Then he strode away from them, aware that everyone in the ballroom was staring at him and that the entire town would be abuzz with what happened in a very short time. Tonight's festivities would be rife with gossip about him and the Gillinghams and, probably, Sadie.

He had to find her. He had to reassure her that he really hadn't intended to marry Lady Frederica, that the only future he wanted was with her.

CHAPTER 12

Unable to endure another moment of the awful spectacle at the pudding competition, Sadie had left the dais and run outside. She'd intended to walk home, but she'd encountered one of the tenants from Fieldstone who'd offered to drive her.

Entering the house, Sadie slammed the door and nearly ran into Mavis in the entrance hall. She was carrying one of Sadie's ball gowns.

"Sadie!" Mavis stared in surprise. "We weren't expecting you. I was going to leave for town in about an hour. Did something happen?"

Sadie wasn't going to explain. She wanted this entire day to just disappear. How could she marry Law after what she'd just witnessed? Lady Frederica—his *actual* betrothed—would be ruined, and Sadie couldn't be a part of that. What's more, she'd fallen for his pretty words, his charming proposal, and been made the fool *again*, with people laughing at her just like four years ago.

Except, unlike with Osborne, Sadie actually believed that Law loved her, that everything between them had been pure and true. And she definitely loved him. However, he was still a duke with responsibilities and expectations he needed to meet. She was now quite sure that him marrying her was *not* expected and would not be welcome. Law would put his ducal duty first—as he should. Sadie would do the same and always had when it came to her family and Fieldstone.

Gwen came into the entrance hall from the other side. She also stopped short and blinked at Sadie. "You aren't supposed to be here."

Sadie's ire spiked. "Why not? I *live* here."

"You just rarely break from your stated routine," Gwen said with a shrug.

That was true. But today was different. Today was horrible, and there was nothing regular or routine about it.

"Are you still going to the gardens tonight?" Mavis asked cautiously.

The door hit Sadie's back, pushing her forward. She grunted and moved to the center of the hall as her father and two older brothers filed in.

Her father looked at her, his brow creasing into deep furrows. "Why aren't you still in town?"

Bryan entered the hall from the back of the house. "Sadie, Mother said you came back with Mrs. Bledsoe. Did you come here instead of staying in town so we could celebrate Mother's best pudding?" He grinned from ear to ear. "She'll be here in a moment. She's just gone to fetch Father."

Sadie was thrilled that Mrs. Rowell had won—or she would be. Later. Now, she was too upset at being a laughingstock once more.

"Is that why you came back?" her father prodded. "You should have stayed in town with the other maidens fair—with the duke."

At the mention of Law, Sadie wanted to run upstairs and throw herself under her bed where she could cry in peace.

"Well, now that Sadie's here, she can help us put together a celebration for Mrs. Rowell," Philip said.

"She can also mend my shirt," Esmond said. "It's my best one, and I want to wear it tonight. Annabelle's too busy with the boys."

"I can mend your shirt," Mavis offered. "If I have time after I spruce up Sadie's dress."

"Why do you have to do that?" Sadie's father asked. He glanced toward the gown in Mavis's arms. "Why can't she wear the new gown you convinced me to buy?"

Anger and frustration swirled around Sadie as she stood in the center of everyone talking. Then Adam and Richard came in the front door, jostling her father and older brothers.

"You'll never guess what happened at the pudding competition," Adam said before his gaze landed on Sadie. He snapped his mouth closed as his eyes widened.

"Yes, do tell everyone what happened," Sadie said softly, but with more anger than she'd ever felt in her life.

"Er, no." Adam shook his head vigorously. He clearly hadn't expected her to be here, but then none of them had. "It's…not important."

It bloody well was.

"What happened?" her father asked, turning toward Adam.

"I'll tell you later," Adam said, his gaze darting to Sadie as he fidgeted with his coat.

Bryan grimaced. "I can tell you, Mr. Campion. An earl showed up with his daughter saying she's to wed His Grace. It will be announced at the ball tomorrow night with the rest of the matches."

Sadie's father's face fell. Then his eyes narrowed, and his jaw clenched in anger. "That blackguard!"

"He's not a blackguard," Sadie murmured. "He's just a duke."

Mrs. Rowell and her husband entered, and it was, by far, the most people who had ever squeezed into the entrance hall. "Bryan, I told you to keep that to yourself." The cook sent Sadie an apologetic glance. Of course she'd heard everything that had gone on. Or at least most of it. Along with everyone else in the ballroom.

"Well then, let's definitely have a celebration for Mrs. Rowell," Adam said enthusiastically. "It will cheer Sadie up!"

"No!" Sadie had never shouted so loudly. She squeezed her eyes shut for a brief moment, then opened them to look at everyone gathered around her. "I don't want to plan a party or mend a shirt or be cheered up. I don't want to answer any of your bloody questions, and I don't want your pity about the duke. I'd like to be *alone* for once. Is that too much to ask?"

"No," a few of them answered quietly.

But Sadie wasn't finished. She looked to her father. "You've shamelessly thrown me at the duke since his arrival after never showing the slightest interest in whether I wed. You've never even discussed hiring a new housekeeper since Mrs. Evans died!"

Sadie's father blinked at her, nonplussed. "Why do we need a housekeeper? Everything seems to get done."

He was flanked by Philip and Richard, who both elbowed him. If Sadie hadn't been so furious, she would have laughed. Or thanked them. Or both.

"We've taken you for granted," Richard said, looking at her with a sad expression.

"Yes." Sadie felt tears welling in her throat and

behind her eyes. She was *not* going to cry in front of them. "And I'm not going to tolerate it any longer." Holding her head up, she strode toward the back of the hall. Mrs. Rowell and Bryan immediately parted to allow her to pass.

Sadie stalked up the stairs and went straight to her room, slamming the door closed after she stepped inside. Now the tears fell. She wiped at them angrily, hating that she'd fallen for a shallow man and his empty words a second time.

Instead of ducking under her bed, she went to the mirror and looked at her reddened cheeks and her puffy eyes. She was going to need several cold cloths to ensure she would look unaffected at the festival tonight.

She couldn't hide here at Fieldstone as she'd done the last time. As a maiden fair, she had an obligation, and dammit, she wasn't going to let a man's perfidy dictate her behavior.

Lifting her chin, she glimpsed the strong woman everyone said she was, the woman who would rise above this setback. As if it wasn't a crushing devastation.

~

Law had gone back into the pudding competition and completed his voting, reasoning that would be less controversial than if he'd simply abandoned his duties after the spectacle. No one mentioned what happened—to their credit—but Sadie's absence weighed on him like a massive stone.

Mrs. Rowell had won the overall competition, but Law didn't stay to congratulate her, nor did he seek to ride back to Fieldstone with her and Bryan. Instead, he walked back, sticking to fields and avoiding the road lest they offer to pick him up.

Perhaps he was being cowardly, but the truth was that he didn't want to talk to anyone but Sadie. He recalled the horrible scene that had unfolded in the assembly rooms, and he wished he'd handled things differently. Except he wasn't sure how that would have been possible. The arrival of Gillingham and Lady Frederica was just an unfortunate occurrence, and it was entirely Yates's fault. Law looked forward to informing the man that he was no longer employed.

When he finally entered the house, he encountered Richard and Gwen speaking in low tones in the staircase hall. They looked toward him, their features creased with uncertainty and concern.

"Where is Sadie?" he asked, sounding surprisingly calm despite the riot of emotions he was experiencing.

"Ah, she's upstairs," Richard said. As Law moved forward, intent on seeing her, the lad raised his hand. "I wouldn't disturb her. She's…upset."

"That might be understating things," Gwen warned. "I've never seen her so angry."

Richard smiled faintly. "That's because you never ruined a bunch of pillows and bedding by leaving it outside in a rainstorm overnight." He sobered. "But yes, she has rarely ever been that upset."

Law tried to imagine Sadie with her ire up, her voice raised. "She actually lost her temper?" He felt even worse, which he didn't think was possible.

Richard nodded. "With everyone. But we deserved it. We've taken her for granted for far too long. Some of us more than others."

So, it hadn't just been about Law? He needed to talk to her more than ever. "I'll go talk to her."

Gwen pursed her lips. "I doubt she'll want to see you, Your Grace. We know what happened at the pudding competition, that you're betrothed to some other lady."

"I'm *not* betrothed." Well, he was—to Sadie. Or at least he hoped he still was.

There was only one way to find out.

Law strode past Richard and Gwen. When he reached Sadie's room, he took a deep breath. Then he lifted his hand and rapped gently. "Sadie? It's Law."

There was a long moment of silence before he finally heard a response. "What do you want?"

He heard the lilt of emotion in her voice and rested his head against the wood. "To see how you are. I'm so sorry about what happened. But I've taken care of things with Gillingham."

The door opened, and he nearly pitched forward. Staggering slightly, he managed to keep his balance. He immediately noted the stiff set of her mouth and the shadow in her eyes.

"I'm tired, and I need to get ready soon for tonight's festivities. That's how I am. It's good that you've come as I have something I need to say."

He hoped she would unburden herself however she needed to. "May I come in?" he asked.

"For a few minutes." She did not close the door entirely after he stepped inside.

Law wasn't sure how to take that, but hoped it didn't mean anything except that she was in haste. Though he burned to reassure her that all was well and that he was definitely *not* marrying Lady Frederica, he wanted her to speak first.

Sadie looked pale as she clasped her hands together. She inhaled deeply before saying, "I can't marry you."

It was as if the wheel had fallen of the coach

again. All the air left Law's lungs, leaving him gasping for breath. The world tilted sideways, and he wondered what had just happened. "I'm sorry, I'm not sure I heard you correctly."

"I'm not marrying you," she repeated. Firmly. Unclasping her hands, she let her arms fall to her sides as color returned to her face. "I worried that being a duchess would make me uncomfortable, and today's...spectacle has confirmed that I prefer the simplicity of my current status."

The sensation of falling—relentlessly—made Law think the floor had disappeared beneath his feet. "I can understand that," he said slowly, trying to work through his thoughts and emotions, which were quite overwhelming in that moment. More than that, he wanted to hear her thoughts and emotions. "I'm so sorry that happened. It was horrible. The Gillinghams were misled as to my intentions. My valet wrote them a letter saying I was eager to wed Lady Frederica, which is, as you know, not true. At least, I hope you know that. I meant what I told you last night. I've no intention of marrying her. I love you. I want to marry *you*."

"I do believe you, but the things the earl said—about his daughter being ruined and the gossip that would follow you—sound very complicated and terrible. I would rather not be a part of that. Today reminded me too much of how I was humiliated four years ago. I have to think that would happen regularly if I were to become your duchess. I don't know the first thing about how to behave in London Society. Add in the fact that everyone will be whispering about me, I've no desire to learn either. Please know that I do love you. I just don't love your title or, more accurately, your place in Society. It's not for me."

Law began to see why she was the woman he'd

fallen in love with. She saw him, not his pedigree. "I would give it all up for you if I could," he said sadly.

"But you can't."

No, he could not. While he could cast off his father's influence, he would still be the Duke of Lawford with all the duties that came with it.

"Everything we've shared has been real to me. You're the best person I've ever known, and though we've only known each other a handful of days, I can't imagine my life without you in it. What about last night?" Law asked. "What if there's a child?"

Surprise flashed in her gaze, but she didn't appear to hold onto the emotion. "It's unlikely there will be after just one encounter. Please don't badger me about it. I don't wish to make problems that aren't there."

"But you would tell me?"

"Of course. Now, if you'll excuse me, I need to bathe and get ready for this evening."

That she was going to attend the festival on her own, to face everyone after what had happened, was a testament to her strength and courage. He wasn't the least bit surprised by her decision to continue on. "You astonish me," he said reverently. "I will deeply regret not having the chance to be the man who stands at your side, who's privileged to call you his wife and his love. And I feel certain I will love you for the rest of my days." He smiled sadly. "I only want you to be happy, and for that reason, I will retreat." He bowed. "My lady maiden fair."

Turning, he left her chamber and wondered just what in the hell he was supposed to do now.

CHAPTER 13

Mavis had been uncharacteristically quiet as she'd dressed Sadie and styled her hair. Sadie had confided in her that morning that Law had asked her to marry him, but had sworn her to secrecy. They hadn't discussed it since.

As Sadie donned her gloves before going downstairs to leave for the gardens with her father and younger brothers, Mavis broke her silence. "Are you not marrying His Grace, then?"

"No, I'm not. The life of a duchess is not for me. I want a simple life with a home and a family. I wouldn't know how to navigate London Society, and honestly, I don't care to learn." If she said it and thought it enough, this would become true, wouldn't it? She could ignore the real truth, that she was afraid to leave the comfort of the place and people she knew, the environment that she managed and adored.

Mavis appeared nearly as crestfallen as Law had earlier. Sadie flinched thinking of that moment, of the hurt in his eyes. That hadn't been her intent. She was trying to avoid her own further hurt and humiliation. And yet, letting him go was as painful

—more so, really—than how she'd felt following the scene at the pudding competition. Still, it was the right thing to do.

"You would be an excellent duchess," Mavis said. "And I would have been with you—a bit of home at your side."

Sadie had asked her to be her lady's maid that morning after telling her about the betrothal. Mavis had been thrilled, particularly since she'd developed an affection for Holden that was reciprocated.

"You would have made it easier, I'm sure," Sadie said. "However, I'm not willing to endure the gossip, and I do feel bad about how this debacle will affect Lady Frederica's reputation."

"None of it was her fault. None of it was the duke's fault either, as far as I can tell," Mavis said.

"It seems like a big misunderstanding, but unfortunately, those can have repercussions—at least in Society. Do you see why I'd choose to stay far away?"

"I suppose." Mavis didn't sound completely convinced. She did, however, sound as if she was done voicing any opposition.

Sadie gave her a faint, sympathetic smile. "If you decide you want to leave Fieldstone, I'll understand. I want you to make the best choice for *you*, just as I've done for me."

"Thank you, Sadie. I don't know what I'll do."

Sadie would be incredibly sad to lose her, but she would never ask her to stay. "I must be on my way." Glancing in the mirror, she looked pale, and her eyes seemed…sad. She needed to find some cheer before arriving at the botanical gardens.

"You're brave to go tonight," Mavis said.

"Thank you. I appreciate you saying that. I've a

duty as a maiden fair, and I'm not going to abandon it."

"You're going to ignore the gossip then and hold your head high. I'm proud of you."

Sadie started toward the door, then nearly caught her foot on the threshold as she realized what Mavis had just done. She'd neatly shown Sadie that she *was* going to endure gossip, that she could very well do that in London as well. If she wanted to.

Well, damn.

Looking back over her shoulder, Sadie gave Mavis a small smile as she narrowed her eyes. "You're very clever, Mavis. I'd be loath to lose you, but Holden will be very lucky."

As Sadie reached the bottom of the stairs, her father coughed. "You look lovely, Sadie. You remind me of your mother, bless her soul."

Sadie froze for a moment. He didn't mention her mother often anymore, and Sadie couldn't recall him ever saying she reminded him of her. "I hope that's a comfort to you, Papa," she said quietly.

"It is. I want you to know how sorry I am about how things are here at Fieldstone. I should have realized you were overburdened."

She felt bad for losing her temper the way she did. "To be fair, I didn't complain. I don't usually mind. It's just that this week, being a maiden fair, I realized how much I do and how much I'd rather do it in my own household."

"I can understand and appreciate that. I've done you a grave disservice not seeing to your marriage before now." He shook his head. "We've all—*I've* come to depend on you so much. I've been selfish, but no more. I spoke to Mrs. Rowell about a potential housekeeper. She has a friend who was working for a vicar who died, and she needs a new position."

"That sounds promising," Sadie said.

He offered her his arm. "Come, Adam and Richard are already in the coach."

They made their way outside, and her father handed her into the vehicle. Bryan had them on their way in a trice.

Both Adam and Richard tried not to look at Sadie. "I'm not angry with you anymore," she said.

They visibly relaxed. "What about the duke?" Adam asked. "The wagers at the Wheatsheaf were nearly all in favor of him proposing."

"I thought you might make a nice wedded couple," Richard said.

Sadie's insides twisted. She'd thought so too. Had she made a mistake? Of course not. She'd made a reasonable choice, one that would ensure she was happy. Even if she wasn't today.

Stiffening her spine against the squab, she said, "I wouldn't want to be a duchess. Can you imagine having to swan about London and meet the queen?" That actually terrified Sadie to a certain extent. What if she embarrassed herself?

"I think it sounds marvelous," Adam said, his eyes shining in the lamplight.

"Think of the scientific lectures I could attend." Richard let out a wistful sigh.

Well, now Sadie felt badly that she wouldn't be able to invite her brothers to visit her in London. But she couldn't make a decision based on them—hadn't she been doing that, putting her family before her own wishes, for far too long? "Perhaps the two of you should move to London."

Their eyes widened briefly, and they turned their heads to look out the window.

"I prefer a simple life in the country with my own modest home," Sadie added.

"Don't overlook the importance of love," their father said, surprising everyone, judging by how they all swung their gazes toward him. "Sometimes it's better to think with your heart instead of your head." A faint smile curled his lips as if he were remembering a distant memory.

"Is that what you did with our mother?" Richard asked.

"Always," he responded with a laugh. "But what's remarkable is that probably for the only time in her life she did the same. Your mother was far more practical than I am." He looked toward Sadie, his gaze holding hers for a moment. "Never underestimate the fortitude of love. It can make anything possible."

It made Sadie think foolishness was more likely —she'd allowed herself to be swept away by Osborne and then Law. It was far better for her to be as practical as her mother was. That gave her comfort. She'd ignore the fact that her mother had apparently followed her heart to wed Sadie's father.

They drove into town and disembarked at the gate to the gardens. She took her father's arm as they entered.

As they neared the central area where the dais was located, Mr. Stackhouse approached her. He bowed. "Good evening, Miss Campion. Might we take a promenade?"

"Certainly." Sadie was glad for the distraction of his company. She took his arm, and they walked toward one of the follies.

"You look lovely tonight."

Sadie was aware that she was wearing the same gown as the first night, but then he hadn't been here to see it. "Thank you." She searched for a topic of conversation. "Where is it you're lodging in town?"

"The Wheatsheaf. It was quite busy this afternoon. Someone told me it was because of the betting book. People were rushing to make new wagers based on—" Color rushed into his face, and he cast an apologetic look at her. "Never mind."

"It's all right," Sadie said, hearing Mavis's words about her courage for enduring the gossip tonight. "I realize what happened at the pudding competition will be a popular topic of discussion this evening." And perhaps for some time.

"I imagine it's awkward for you since the duke is your houseguest." Was that all he meant? Had he not realized that many had suspected she and the duke were courting?

"I'm trying not to pay too close attention," she said vaguely. "I do consider the duke a friend, but that is all." There, she'd addressed any concerns he might have about a potential courtship. She felt Stackhouse relax—she hadn't even realized he was tense, but now it was clear he had been—and an easy smile split his mouth.

"He's very lucky to have a friend such as you," Stackhouse said.

"I can't imagine how he's feeling after what happened." Indeed, she hadn't even asked, and she regretted not doing so. Regardless of what had transpired, they *were* friends. She'd been too focused on telling him she couldn't marry him and his reaction to that.

"Must be awfully complicated being a duke. All the responsibilities and expectations, not to mention the gossip." He waved his hand. "I'm glad not to have such concerns."

"I suppose we all have those things to a certain extent." For some reason, Sadie felt a need to defend Law, which was silly since she'd refused him precisely because she hadn't wanted to join his sophisticated life.

"Yes, I suppose we do. Shall we explore the folly?" he asked.

"That sounds pleasant." Sadie looked askance at Mr. Stackhouse and wondered what she might say if he proposed tomorrow on the last day of the festival, when most proposals took place. That would be a very fast courtship since Stackhouse had arrived late.

How many couples actually fell in love during the whirlwind of the festival? She'd never considered that before. She'd honestly never given the notion of love much thought until this week when it had taken her completely by surprise. Even with Osborne, she hadn't thought she'd fallen in love with him despite expecting he would propose.

But she did love Law.

Her father's words came back to her. Could she allow her heart to guide her?

No, she didn't want that life. She wanted simplicity and comfort. In time, the pain of refusing Law would fade.

CHAPTER 14

After watching Sadie leave in the coach with her father and brothers, Law turned from his window and stared at the bed where just last night he'd made love to Sadie and dreamed of their future together. How had everything come apart so badly and so fast?

But then how had they fallen in love so quickly? He'd never spared much thought for love. Duty was what came to mind when he contemplated marriage. Now, he wasn't sure how to marry someone he *didn't* love. And he couldn't imagine loving anyone other than Sadie.

She'd made it clear she didn't love him, or at least not enough to marry him. The pain of her rejection stung, even if he understood why she'd done it.

Glancing about his room, he wondered where the hell Yates was. Law hadn't seen him since before he'd gone to the pudding competition. Had the man heard Gillingham was in town and run off upon realizing Law would now know of his treachery? No, more likely he was just sulking in his room.

Law left his chamber and went upstairs in

search of the valet. Finding Yates's room empty, Law went to Holden's and rapped on the door.

"Come in." Holden was standing in front of the mirror trying to tie his cravat. He muttered a curse as Law stepped inside.

"That looks awfully difficult to accomplish with one hand." Law moved toward him. "May I help?"

Holden arched a dark brow. "I'm not sure it's acceptable for a duke to knot his coachman's neckcloth."

Law shrugged. "I've decided the expectations for a duke are absurd. I'm going to make my own rules from now on." He did his best to tie the linen into a semblance of a cravat. "I'm quite rubbish at this, which is unfortunate considering I'm going to be without a valet."

"Are you? Is that why I haven't seen Yates all afternoon?"

"I haven't given him his notice yet. I've been wondering where he is." Law surveyed his work. "That will do, I suppose. Who's been managing this for you the past few days?"

Color stained the man's full cheeks. "Mavis. I'm expecting her shortly so we may be on our way to the festival. I thought it would be nice to greet her without having to ask her to finish helping me dress for once."

"I see. It seems you and Mavis have formed an attachment. Is it anything...lasting?"

"I hope it might be. I was, ah, going to speak with you about whether there might be a place for her in one of your households."

Law instantly thought of how losing her would affect Sadie. He didn't want to deprive her of her maid, but neither did he want to prevent the course of true love. "I'm sure there would be—if that's what you want. Let me know once you and Mavis decide."

Holden met his gaze and nodded. "I will, Your Grace. Thank you." His attention shifted to the doorway. "There's Yates now."

Law spun about and went to the door. "Yates!"

The valet was nearly to his room when he stopped. Turning, he summoned a humorless smile. "Your Grace, there you are." He walked toward Holden's room, his frame rigid. "I stopped at your chamber, but you weren't there."

"And where have you been?" Law demanded.

"In town at Lord Gillingham's request. He was hoping there might be an avenue for reconciliation between you and Lady Frederica."

"Reconciliation? I'd never even met her until today." Law took a step toward the older man, his lip curling.

"That may be the case, but your union has been anticipated for months."

"Not by me. I never should have agreed to my father's demands, but I only said I'd consider a betrothal. Any promise made was not by me. But you know that because you forged a letter. How in the hell did you even send a letter during the festival?"

"I walked to another village and paid to have it delivered." He sounded proud of himself.

"That must have cost a great deal." Law hoped so. "I could have you arrested for impersonating me."

Yates twitched as his lips pressed together so tightly that they nearly disappeared.

Holden rushed to the doorway, his eyes wide. "He didn't!"

"He did," Law said tightly. "He wrote a letter in my name saying I was eager to wed Lady Frederica and sent it to her father. He invited them to join me at this matchmaking festival, the perfect place for us to sign a marriage contract. Then they came here expecting a betrothal. Have you any idea what damage you may have caused to Lady Frederica?" Law thundered, disliking that in his ire, he sounded too much like his father.

Yates paled. "There would be no harm if you simply married her. That's the easiest and best solution. It's also what your father wanted."

Law shook his head. "You've no remorse at all, do you?"

"Where is *your* remorse?" Yates's eyes goggled. "You've been carrying on with that…with Miss Campion here instead of making your way to Lord Gillingham's estate. It's a travesty."

A white-hot anger burned in Law's chest when he thought of what word Yates might have used to describe Sadie. "You'd best watch yourself," he growled, seething.

Yates sneered. "I watch everything and everyone. Why can't you see I've been trying to help you? If only I'd been able to keep you away from her." He pressed his lips together as if he were trying not to speak.

Law froze. "What did you *do*?" His red face, the malaise after the picnic, which he was now entirely certain had been laudanum. "You drugged me." Law gaped at the man, shocked at his depravity.

The valet went stiff. "I did what was necessary. And there was no harm done."

Law shook with fury. "You've caused plenty of harm, and you don't care because it was in the name of serving my father. You will earn no favor from a dead man, nor will you receive any from me. You are dismissed effective immediately—without reference."

Now Yates turned gray. "But, Your Grace, I've been a loyal retainer for decades."

"Your loyalty was entirely to my father, as you just demonstrated. I've no need for someone like you in my employ. Furthermore, I can't in good conscience recommend you given what you've done. You're lucky I don't seek Mr. Sneed to take you into custody."

"How am I to go on?" Yates whined.

"I'm sure I don't know. Perhaps Lord Gillingham can help you. I suggest you pack your things and seek him out before he leaves Marry-well. I'd also recommend you don't drug him."

Yates's lips flapped for a moment before he turned and scurried into his bedchamber, slam-ming the door with a loud thud.

"That was brilliant. Did he actually drug you?" Holden asked, incredulous.

"After the picnic, I returned here and had tea. I collapsed into bed shortly thereafter, and I would have sworn I'd taken laudanum. Apparently, I did. I should have realized it then." Law was supremely annoyed with himself for not seeing the valet for the threat that he was.

"And he purposely turned your face red? Was that to keep you from escorting Miss Campion to the festival?"

"It seems so." Law wondered if he ought to have the man arrested after all. He was a menace.

Holden gave him a firm nod. "I never liked him. No one in the stables does. Most of the London household can't stand him either. And probably half the folks at Hedgeley." He referred to Law's ducal estate.

"I didn't realize that. How are you all so good at hiding your opinions?"

Holden shrugged. "That's just what we do, especially, and I beg your pardon, with an employer like your father."

"Well, I should like to know about disruptive retainers. I hope Yates wasn't too terrible." Given what he'd done with the forgery, Law wondered what other dastardly deeds he'd done.

"Just aggressively annoying," Holden said.

"He is that." Law exhaled. "I suppose this means I'll need to pack my own things. I'd expected that, of course. I'll do that while you are at the festival tonight. Then we can leave in the morning."

"So soon?"

Dammit. Law should have thought of how that would affect Holden and his courtship of the maid. "I realize that doesn't give you much time, however, I can't stay here at Fieldstone. After you drive me back to London, you can take some time away and return, if that's acceptable."

"That's most generous, but why are you leaving? What about Miss Campion?"

Before Law could respond, Mavis appeared at the top of the stairs. She came toward them, her brow pleating. "Why are you standing in the corridor?" Her gaze settled on Holden, and she smiled. "You tied your neckcloth."

"His Grace did, actually."

Mavis shifted her attention to Law. "That was very kind of you, Your Grace." She gave him a sad, sympathetic look. "I'm sorry about what happened today."

"No sorrier than I am."

"I hope I'm not speaking out of turn, but I think you should know that Sadie told me about your proposal. She was so happy this morning, happier than I've ever seen her. I can't believe she's changed her mind."

Holden's eyes rounded. "Wait, you were betrothed, and now she's throwing you over?"

"She's making a better choice for herself. She doesn't wish to complicate her life by becoming a duchess. I can't say that I blame her."

"I can't either," Mavis said with a slight frown. "I do think she'll end up regretting it, though."

She did? And wouldn't she know? Mavis had been working at Fieldstone for many years, if Law remembered correctly from one of his many conversations with Sadie.

"Does she love him?" Holden asked Mavis.

Mavis nodded. "I'm sure she does."

Holden looked to Law. "And you love her?"

"More than anything."

"Then why aren't you fighting for her?" Holden asked, his brows pitched into a deep V.

"Because she was very clear in her rejection. I must respect her wishes."

Holden waved his hand. "Bah, not if she's upset and likely to regret her decision. I wouldn't give up so easily."

It was difficult not to feel a surge of hope. Perhaps he had surrendered too quickly. He did love her, and she'd said just last night that she loved him. Surely, she wouldn't have changed her mind. Except she had—about marrying him.

He thought of all the times his father had forced him to do things again and again until he overcame his fear or mastered the skill. Perhaps that was what he needed to do here.

Of course it was. The realization made Law smile. If his father had known all that would have prepared him for this—to marry a woman of whom he would not approve—he might never have demanded so much.

Law would try to persuade Sadie to overcome

her anxiety about being his duchess. He just had to show her that hiding at Fieldstone would not make her as happy as them being together, conquering their fears and sharing their responsibilities—and their love.

Law looked from Holden to Mavis. "How can I prove to her that we belong together?"

Mavis smiled. "What does Sadie want most of all?"

There was no need to even think of the answer. It just tumbled from Law's mouth. "A home. Family. And *not* in London as a duchess," he added drily. Suddenly, he knew what he had to do. The solution was obvious. But would she agree with him?

"I need to go to the festival," he said, anxious to be on his way immediately.

"We were going to walk since I don't know how to drive and Holden can't," Mavis said. "But I believe the gig is here. Can you hitch it up?"

"I could put my own team on my own coach if I had to, but the gig is easier if you think we can all squeeze in there together."

"Mavis can sit on my lap," Holden said with a grin.

She swatted his arm. "Rogue! I have made you no promises."

"His Grace has said he'll find a place for you, if you would consent to be my wife."

Lovely pink roses bloomed in Mavis's cheeks. "Sadie was going to bring me as her lady's maid. I confess I was ecstatic when she told me, then devastated when she changed her mind."

Law gave the maid a level stare. "With luck, I'm going to persuade her to be my duchess, and then she will most definitely need a lady's maid. All will work out as it should."

He prayed that would be true.

~

After promenading with Stackhouse, Sadie returned to her father and brothers for a short while. Then Mr. Atkins had come to ask for another promenade, and they'd made a circuit of the main area around the dais. Both gentlemen were kind, in possession of precisely the kind of home she would like to call her own and would make fine husbands. Neither of them, however, were Law.

Atkins delivered her back to her father and took his leave with a bow. "Remember to save me that dance later," he said with a smile.

"Is that boy old enough to marry?" her father asked when Atkins was out of earshot.

"He just looks young," Sadie replied. "He's actually two years older than I am."

Her father narrowed one eye at her. "Does he wish to court you?" He'd asked her the same thing after she'd promenaded with Stackhouse.

"He said he looks forward to spending time with me. He asked me to dance later and suggested we walk through the labyrinth."

"Harrumph." Her father appeared disgruntled. "Nothing good ever happens in the labyrinth."

Sadie stared at him. "You've never once said that. What would you say if I was going there with the duke?" She *had* gone there with him, and it had been everything good. And wonderful. And absolutely incomparable.

"I would lead you there myself," her father said without a hint of irony.

Sadie rolled her eyes.

"What was wrong with him?" her father asked. "The duke, I mean."

"Nothing was wrong with *him*." On the contrary, he made her feel desirable and important. He'd called her the best person he knew. How could she not find him wonderful in return?

Then why aren't you marrying him?

Again, she wondered if she was making a mistake and if her father's counsel was worth her attention. Thankfully, it was nearly time to go onto the dais with the other maidens fair.

Glancing toward the short stairs that led up to the dais, she saw Law walking with the mayor. Law looked so handsome in his evening wear with his crisp black coat and his snowy white cravat. Sadie tilted her head to the side. That was not his typical knot. His blond hair ruffled slightly in the breeze, and she recalled the silken feel of it between her fingers. She remembered all of him pressed against her, and a rush of heat suffused her.

He and Armstrong ascended onto the dais together. What was going on?

Armstrong strode toward the front where he typically spoke while Law hung slightly back, his gaze moving over the crowd.

"Good evening, Marrywellers and guests!" Armstrong said loudly enough to carry over the wide lawn. "I'm joined here on the dais by our esteemed guest, His Grace, the Duke of Lawford. I'm delighted to announce that the duke is so smitten with our charming village that he plans to stay indefinitely!"

Sadie gasped, and she realized it was just one of hundreds of the same sound. A low buzz carried as people responded to one another regarding this news.

"Well, that's bloody unexpected," Adam said.

Yes, it was. Sadie didn't think she could breathe.

"His Grace will be seeking to purchase an appropriate property nearby, one that will provide additional lodging for guests during the festival, which means an expansion of our attendance!"

That would bring additional funds to their town, which relied on the festival. Why was he doing this?

"The duke would like to say a few words." Armstrong gestured for Law to join him at the front of the dais.

Law moved forward, and in that instant, his eyes locked with Sadie's. "I have absolutely fallen in love with Marrywell," he said. Sadie's heart flipped, and now she absolutely could *not* breathe. He looked past her and scanned the large gathering, but she kept her gaze fixed on him. "I look forward to calling this beautiful place my home. One of them anyway. While I do have duties that require me to be in London during the Season, I'll be here as much as I can, especially during the festival." He looked directly at her again, and it seemed as though he was speaking to her and her alone.

"Listen to that," Sadie's father said softly. "He's fallen in love with our town."

Sadie glanced over at him to see he was looking at her instead of the dais. He arched a brow and wore a decidedly smug expression.

She swung her gaze back to the dais. Law was going to make Marrywell his home? Well, one of his homes. Why would he do that after she rejected him?

Because he's not giving up.

She'd told him she didn't want to be a duchess, that she preferred her simple life. He would do everything he could—within the bounds of his own duty—to give her exactly that. At least, she thought that was what he was saying.

Law smiled at her from the dais, and her heart lodged in her throat. She loved him so much. Her father was right. Sometimes it was best to listen to one's heart.

Armstrong announced that it was time for the queen, king, and maidens fair to join him on the dais. Sadie made her way to the stairs, her legs feeling slightly wobbly. At least, she was breathing again.

She climbed onto the dais, following behind the other maidens who filed past the mayor. When she reached him, Sadie paused. "Could you have the duke ask me his question again?" she whispered.

Armstrong's brow creased in confusion.

"Just ask him if he will," Sadie said, clenching her hands into fists and releasing them as a heady anticipation fluttered through her.

Turning, Armstrong went back to Law. "Miss Campion would like to know if you'd ask her your question again."

Law's gaze met hers. He arched a brow, and she saw the question in his expression.

She nodded, a slight smile curving her lips.

"I would be delighted," Law said softly. He sank to one knee and more loudly asked, "Miss Campion, would you do me the honor of becoming my duchess?"

"I will." A grin overtook her, and she began to shake with emotion.

The gardens erupted with applause and cheers. Sadie felt wetness on her cheeks, but it wasn't raining, of course.

Law came forward and took her in his arms. He kissed her forehead and caressed her cheek. "I'm so glad you said yes."

"How could I say no to *that* proposal?" She shook her head and wiped the back of her gloved hand over her cheeks. "It wasn't just the proposal. I had already started to regret changing my mind. Did you mean what you said about living here?"

"Of course I did. I can't keep you from being a duchess, but I can give you the home, the place, and anything else your heart desires."

"What my heart desires most is you," she said, touching his face. "I really don't need a fourth house here in Marrywell. Just promise we'll visit Fieldstone often and try to always attend the Matchmaking Festival."

"We can discuss the fourth house—I am entirely smitten with your town. I promise we'll come back to your home as much as you want, and there is no way I'm missing a festival. I want to kiss you, but I'm afraid that would be too much of a spectacle." He gave her a wicked smile. "But I promise to do that and much more later when we are alone. If you'll allow it."

She gave him a saucy look. "You know me well enough by now to expect that I'll demand it."

He laughed, then kissed her temple. "And yours are the only demands I care about."

"Huzzah!" Armstrong shouted. "What a start to night six! We have our first betrothal, and what a spectacular one it is. Let us congratulate His Grace, the Duke of Lawford, and our very own Miss Sadie Campion!"

There were more cheers, and Sadie felt as if she might burst from happiness. She looked out over the sea of faces and was overcome with joy. "This exceeds anything I imagined." She looked at Law. "You've made dreams I didn't even know I had come true."

"Then you'd best dream up some more so I can bring those to reality too."

"Let us commence the dancing," Armstrong announced. "Led by our newly betrothed couple!"

Sadie took Law's arm, and they left the dais. Her entire family was waiting at the bottom of the stairs.

"That was the most romantic thing I've ever seen," Annabelle said, wiping her nose with a handkerchief.

Law moved to Sadie's father. "I should have asked your permission first. I hope you can forgive me."

"You're marrying my daughter!" Sadie's father sniffed. "Are you really going to live here in Marrywell? Or were you just trying to convince Sadie to wed you?"

"Yes, Sadie and I will spend as much time here as we can."

"We'll discuss it," Sadie said. "I realize that if I can manage four brothers and my father and a bustling household, I can likely handle being a duchess. How difficult can London Society be?"

"That is quite a change of attitude," Law whispered near her ear. "I believe you can do anything you set your mind to. And I'll make sure all of London knows what a wonderful, capable, astonishingly clever woman you are."

She looked up at him. "I was afraid, and I don't want to be. I don't think I can be with you at my side." Grinning, she tugged him toward the dance floor. "Come, we need to dance."

"You're welcome at Fieldstone any time!" her father called after them.

The mayor announced a waltz in celebration of Sadie and Law's betrothal. Law took her into his arms as the music started. They were alone for now, but the other members of the court would join them shortly.

"You really aren't afraid anymore?" Law asked.

"I know there will be challenges, but I am up to them. There is just one thing, however. Will Lady Frederica be all right? I'm quite upset thinking she may be ruined."

Law gave her a reassuring squeeze as they moved with the music. "She should be fine. There may be some gossip, but it won't be as dire as Gillingham made it sound. If he waits until next Season to launch her, I predict she'll be quite successful."

"Would it help if I paid her special attention? Perhaps we could make her a special guest at a ball or something." Sadie gave him a lopsided smile. "Honestly, I've no idea how any of that works."

"You shall sort it out, and you can set a new style for doing things." He looked at her intently. "I believe very strongly that you will be the most successful duchess London has ever seen."

Sadie felt as though she were glowing with love. "Your faith in me is all I really need. I should have realized that sooner. I'm so sorry I rejected you."

"You've no need to apologize. I fully understand why you changed your mind. What happened at the pudding competition was truly awful. I am pleased to report that Yates is no longer in my employ. Can you believe he turned my face red on purpose, and he put laudanum in my tea—all to keep me from attending the festival with you?"

She gaped at him. "The blackguard!"

"Quite. I shall need to hire a new valet. But you already have a lady's maid—Mavis will be thrilled that you've changed your mind, as she and Holden would like to be married."

"Truly?" Sadie didn't think she could get even happier, but she did.

"Truly." He guided her expertly as the others joined them in the dance. "I'm just glad I was able to keep my promise to you."

Sadie laughed softly. "That I'd be betrothed by the end of the festival?"

He nodded. "And I've a day to spare."

"I claim it as mine," Sadie said, looking up at him with seductive intent.

"You may have all my days, my dearest love. Until the end of time."

EPILOGUE

One year later

"You are so handsome. Yes, you are." Sadie kissed her son's head as she balanced him on her lap. She loved the smell of his pale downy hair. At two months old, Jerome was full of smiles and laughter and, occasionally, gas. But even then, he had her entire heart—along with his father. Sadie's gaze darted to where Law stood with her father sipping brandy.

"When do you need to leave for the welcome reception?" Sadie's father asked.

As expected, Law and Sadie were this year's May King and Queen. However, they were not staying at the New Inn, nor had they managed to purchase a house near Marrywell. They'd been too busy settling into married life, and Sadie had wanted to spend time at the houses that Law already owned.

All that meant that Sadie was able to spend time at Fieldstone, which was thriving under the care of the new housekeeper, Mrs. Fitz, along with two new maids.

In her late forties, Amelia Fitz was a petite Black woman with a kind smile and an iron will. No one questioned her authority or expertise at Fieldstone. In many ways, she'd improved things, in that no one expected her to do things for them that they could—and should—do for themselves. Sadie adored her.

As if summoned by Sadie's thoughts, Mrs. Fitz came into the parlor. "There is food in the dining room for anyone who'd care to eat before going to the welcome reception."

Sadie's father immediately stood taller. He moved toward Mrs. Fitz. "You do think of everything. I wonder how we ever managed without you."

It took a monumental effort for Sadie not to roll her eyes, but since arriving nearly a week ago, she'd deduced that her father was smitten with Mrs. Fitz—something Sadie hadn't noticed when they'd visited for a fortnight during Yuletide. Sadie didn't think the woman knew, or if she did, she was very good at playing ignorant. Or perhaps she wasn't interested.

"Your daughter managed things just fine," Mrs. Fitz scolded. "Don't you go flattering me at her expense." There was a teasing light in her eyes that made Sadie think she actually *might* be interested. Perhaps she ought to choose Mrs. Fitz as a maiden fair.

That led Sadie's stomach to knot. She was nervous about her upcoming task at the welcome reception. How would she pick only seven? Since Sadie was added last year, could she also add maidens this year? She doubted they'd make an exception simply because she was having a hard time making her selections.

"We should probably eat something," Law said, finishing his brandy. Setting the empty glass atop a table, he moved to Sadie. "Are we taking Jerome with us?"

They generally took him everywhere since he was still so small, and Sadie was nursing him. "I think we should bring his nurse in case he falls asleep in the coach. Then he can stay there to finish his nap."

"I can come along too," Mavis said as she came into the parlor. She had just informed Sadie a fortnight earlier that she and Holden would welcome their own child later in the year. "Not that you need me, but I always love spending time with our favorite little man." She smiled at Jerome.

Sadie rose and turned to Mavis. "Actually, would you mind taking him up to the nurse? I'd like to eat something before we get ready to leave."

"I'd be delighted." Mavis took Jerome and murmured nonsensical things as she carried him from the parlor.

Sadie took her husband's arm. "Let us eat." They went to the dining room, where Sadie piled a plate full of Mrs. Rowell's finest—which was everything she cooked.

Law's plate was also overflowing. "By the time we leave, I may be twice the size as when we arrived. It's a good thing she refused my offer to come cook for us."

Gasping, Sadie stared at him as they set their plates on the table. "You didn't really do that?"

He shook his head, laughing. "I made an offer in jest. I know she would never leave Fieldstone. And while I would also have happily employed her husband, I know he's needed here."

"Yes, my father is not the best at managing the estate," Sadie said with a sigh. "But Rowell says Esmond is showing promise, so that's good to hear. I worried he wouldn't ever find the maturity. And Philip has been managing the new property." Her father had purchased it about six months ago. "It seems my brothers are rising to their potential now that I'm not here."

"I believe you inspired them," Law said, holding her chair.

But Sadie didn't sit. She turned and looked at her husband, amazed at how much her life had changed in just a year. "Perhaps, but I think they always had it in them."

"I should think so since you are all made from the same cloth, and you are the most capable, brilliant, exceptional woman in all the world."

"All the world? Goodness, that is hard to believe."

Law stepped around the chair and put his arms around her waist. "You've mastered being a duchess, conquered London Society, and are proving to be the most wonderful mother who ever lived. These are all objective facts." He kissed her cheek, then the space behind her ear.

Sadie laughed as she put her hands on his chest and tilted her head so he could do whatever he liked to her neck, which was where his lips went next. "You are only slightly biased."

He lifted his head and looked into her eyes with a love that made Sadie's heart swell. "I'm not biased. I'm *beguiled*. I am also more in love with you today than yesterday, and I shall be even more in love with you tomorrow. I could never have imagined such a thing, but there you are. It's all because of you."

"It's a little because of you too."

He laughed before kissing her soundly. "Let us eat, my queen, before I decide to ravish you instead."

She narrowed her eyes at him in seductive invitation. "Can't we do both?"

Caressing her cheek, Law smiled. "You are Queen of the May. We can do whatever you command."

Thank you so much for reading Beguiling the Duke. I hope you enjoyed it! Don't miss the next book in Lords in Love by Erica Ridley, **TAMING THE RAKE** :

The ton's worst rake ruined her, now she's back for revenge—and his heart!

Would you like to know when my next book is available and to hear about sales and deals? Sign up for my VIP newsletter, follow me on social media:

Facebook: https://facebook.com/DarcyBurkeFans
Twitter at @darcyburke
Instagram at darcyburkeauthor
Pinterest at darcyburkewrite

And follow me on Bookbub to receive updates on pre-orders, new releases, and deals!

Need more Regency romance? Check out my other historical series:

The Phoenix Club
Society's most exclusive invitation...

Welcome to the Phoenix Club, where London's

most audacious, disreputable, and intriguing ladies and gentlemen find scandal, redemption, and second chances.

Matchmaking Chronicles

The course of true love never runs smooth. Sometimes a little matchmaking is required. When couples meet at a house party, what could go wrong?

The Untouchables

Swoon over twelve of Society's most eligible and elusive bachelor peers and the bluestockings, wallflowers, and outcasts who bring them to their knees!

The Untouchables: The Spitfire Society

Meet the smart, independent women who've decided they don't need Society's rules, their families' expectations, or, most importantly, a husband. But just because they don't need a man doesn't mean they might not *want* one...

The Untouchables: The Pretenders

Set in the captivating world of The Untouchables, follow the saga of a trio of siblings who excel at being something they're not. Can a dauntless Bow Street Runner, a devastated viscount, and a disillusioned Society miss unravel their secrets?

Wicked Dukes Club

Six books written by me and my BFF, NYT Bestselling Author Erica Ridley. Meet the unforgettable men of London's most notorious tavern, The Wicked Duke. Seductively handsome, with charm and wit to spare, one night with these rakes and rogues will never be enough...

Love is All Around

Heartwarming Regency-set retellings of classic Christmas stories (written after the Regency!) featuring a cozy village, three siblings, and the best gift of all: love.

Secrets and Scandals

Six epic stories set in London's glittering ballrooms and England's lush countryside.

Legendary Rogues

Five intrepid heroines and adventurous heroes embark on exciting quests across the Georgian Highlands and Regency England and Wales!

If you like contemporary romance, I hope you'll check out my **Ribbon Ridge** series available from Avon Impulse, and the continuation of Ribbon Ridge in **So Hot**.

I hope you'll consider leaving a review at your favorite online vendor or networking site!

I appreciate my readers so much. Thank you, thank you, *thank you.*

ALSO BY DARCY BURKE

Historical Romance

Lords in Love

Beguiling the Duke by Darcy Burke

Taming the Rake by Erica Ridley

Romancing the Heiress by Darcy Burke

Defying the Earl by Erica Ridley

Matching the Marquess by Darcy Burke

Chasing the Bride by Erica Ridley

The Phoenix Club

Improper

Impassioned

Intolerable

Indecent

Impossible

Irresistible

Impeccable

Insatiable

Matchmaking Chronicles

The Rigid Duke

The Bachelor Earl (also prequel to *The Untouchables*)

The Runaway Viscount

The Make-Believe Widow

The Unexpected Rogue

The Never Duchess

The Untouchables: The Pretenders

A Secret Surrender

A Scandalous Bargain

A Rogue to Ruin

The Untouchables

The Bachelor Earl (prequel)

The Forbidden Duke

The Duke of Daring

The Duke of Deception

The Duke of Desire

The Duke of Defiance

The Duke of Danger

The Duke of Ice

The Duke of Ruin

The Duke of Lies

The Duke of Seduction

The Duke of Kisses

The Duke of Distraction

The Untouchables: The Spitfire Society

Never Have I Ever with a Duke

A Duke is Never Enough

A Duke Will Never Do

Love is All Around

(A Regency Holiday Trilogy)

The Red Hot Earl

The Gift of the Marquess

Joy to the Duke

Wicked Dukes Club

One Night for Seduction by Erica Ridley

One Night of Surrender by Darcy Burke

One Night of Passion by Erica Ridley

One Night of Scandal by Darcy Burke

One Night to Remember by Erica Ridley

One Night of Temptation by Darcy Burke

Secrets and Scandals

Her Wicked Ways

His Wicked Heart

To Seduce a Scoundrel

To Love a Thief (a novella)

Never Love a Scoundrel

Scoundrel Ever After

Legendary Rogues

The Legend of a Rogue (prequel available only to newsletter subscribers)

Lady of Desire

Romancing the Earl

Lord of Fortune

Captivating the Scoundrel

Contemporary Romance

Ribbon Ridge

Where the Heart Is (a prequel novella)

Only in My Dreams

Yours to Hold

When Love Happens

The Idea of You

When We Kiss

You're Still the One

Ribbon Ridge: So Hot

So Good

So Right

So Wrong

Prefer to read in German, French, or Italian? Check out my website for foreign language editions!

ABOUT THE AUTHOR

Darcy Burke is the USA Today Bestselling Author of sexy, emotional historical and contemporary romance. Darcy wrote her first book at age 11, a happily ever after about a swan addicted to magic and the female swan who loved him, with exceedingly poor illustrations. Join her Reader Club newsletter for the latest updates from Darcy.

A native Oregonian, Darcy lives on the edge of wine country with her guitar-strumming husband, artist daughter, and imaginative son who will almost certainly out-write her one day (that may be tomorrow). They're a crazy cat family with two Bengal cats, a small, fame-seeking cat named after a fruit, an older rescue Maine Coon with attitude to spare, an adorable former stray who wandered onto their deck and into their hearts, and two bonded boys who used to belong to (separate) neighbors but chose them instead. You can find Darcy at a winery, in her comfy writing chair balancing her laptop and a cat or three, folding laundry (which she loves), or binge-watching TV with the family. Her happy places are Disneyland, Labor Day weekend at the Gorge, Denmark, and anywhere in the UK—so long as her family is there too. Visit Darcy online at www.darcyburke.com and follow her on social media.

facebook.com/DarcyBurkeFans
twitter.com/darcyburke
instagram.com/darcyburkeauthor
pinterest.com/darcyburkewrites
goodreads.com/darcyburke
bookbub.com/authors/darcy-burke
amazon.com/author/darcyburke

CPSIA information can be obtained
at www.ICGtesting.com
Printed in the USA
LVHW052133070623
749217LV00021B/372